Sam Cheever creates some of the best characters you could ever find in the pages of a book.

— SENSUALREADS.COM

Ms. Cheever writes with class, humor and lots of fun while weaving an excellent story.

— THE ROMANCE STUDIO

This is no boring librarian shushing people from behind a desk. This librarian corrals rogue magic. But more importantly, she has a frog and a cat, and she's not afraid to use them!

I knew when I woke up with a migraine that things were going to get interesting. As a magical artifact wrangler, it's not an unusual way to start my day. But I had no idea how bad it was going to get.

Until I found a frog sitting in my teacup.

Even that, I could explain to myself if I had to. After all, I have a creative mind. But when the frog started talking to me, yeah, I was pretty sure I'd taken the wrong kind of pill that morning for my headache.

If only I'd realized then what I know now. The talking frog was just the beginning of my problems. And quite a beginning it was!

TEA & CROAKIES

SAM CHEEVER

ELECTRIC PROSE PUBLICATIONS

1

BEWARE PINCHING CHAIRS

I've been told from an early age that magic wrangling is a science. Color me skeptical. It's not that I don't believe it's a science. It's that, for me, the whole process is really more of a hit or miss, try until you die proposition. It's like I'm missing something that will make it easier. As if someone forgot to give me my magic wand when I reached my eighteenth birthday and came into my powers.

Or rather, my powers came into me. With a *crash, thump, grab your rump* kind of unexpectedness that left me hanging over the toilet horking and holding my head with both hands as it tried to split in two.

Even now, five years later, I still get the migraines. I wish I could say they've gotten easier over time. And maybe they have. But if you're making a comparison between a tsunami and a level

5 hurricane, it's really a distinction without a whole lot of difference for the people getting pounded by weather. Well, except one might kill you faster.

I'm thinking my shelf life might be a little bit longer these days, though I couldn't prove it.

At the moment, with a thousand tiny gnomes wearing spiked golf shoes and using pickle forks as walking sticks dancing on my brain, I was thinking it might be preferable to die faster anyway.

The world suddenly erupted in a series of explosions which had a familiar cadence to them. I hid under my long, brown hair and fought my lids to get them to open. But they fought back, eventually snapping closed again as the explosions stopped and the door my intruder had been banging on swung slowly open. "Naida? Are you awake?"

All evidence to the contrary, I was, unfortunately, awake. I grunted something even I couldn't decipher and my torturer took it as permission to come into my room.

"I closed up downstairs. Do you want me to make you some tea?"

My lips moved and more words nobody could understand eased through them. Fortunately, my loyal, if slightly annoying, assistant understood Migrainish Gibberish.

"I felt the magic arrive a few minutes ago, so I went ahead and closed up," she cheerfully said as she picked up my teapot and proceeded to bang out the Star-Spangled Banner with it on my stovetop.

Not really, of course. But only because she wasn't musically inclined and couldn't recreate the Star-Spangled Banner if her life depended on it.

"Ugh!" I said, hoping she could interpret that single non-word as "Please try to be quieter. My head is killing me."

Bang! "Oh say..." Crash "...can you see..." Clang "by the dawn's early light..."

"Sebille!"

She jerked to a halt as I sat bolt upright in my bed, my blue eyes flying open with outrage. I immediately regretted the decision to move, my brain pulsing unhappily inside my head and the soldiers with pickle forks breaking into a rowdy rendition of the Irish Chicken Dance. "You're killing me."

True to form, my non-serious friend simply rolled her almost iridescent green eyes. "Drama much?"

I put my head into my hands and groaned. "Why do I bother?"

A steaming mug appeared in front of my face. The sweet, floral scent undulated toward my nostrils in a siren song I could not resist. Taking the mug, I sniffed first, letting the sweet deliciousness infuse my sinuses.

The headache eased a bit just from that sniff,

and by the time I'd drained the mug a few minutes later, the pain was gone.

I sighed. "Are you sure you're not a witch? Tea never works this well when I make it."

Sebille dropped onto the edge of my bed. "You know I'm not a witch. I'm just tea-talented."

I would have sighed but the extra air rushing through my system probably would have enraged the soldiers with pickle forks. "Thank you. I was working up the courage to make myself some when you assaulted my door."

Sebille shook her head. "You always exaggerate so."

I glowered at her. "And you have zero compassion."

Shrugging, she tugged a strand of her bright red hair before tucking it behind a pointed ear. "That is unfortunately true."

No remorse. Which, BTW, perfectly matched her lack of compassion.

"Did you get a read on the wave?" I asked.

My assistant uncrossed a long, bony leg and tucked it underneath her, the other leg dangling over the edge of the bed. She wore her customary green and white striped socks and slightly pointed red shoes, making her look like the Wicked Witch of the West. Well, from the knees down, anyway. "No. But, I did get a sense it was important to Croakies."

Croakies was the name of my shop. Before you ask me why a magical artifact shop would be named Croakies, don't. I couldn't possibly tell you. That was the name of the store when I bought the place from the previous Keeper of the Artifacts. She'd been kind of scattered, seeming more interested in moving onto her next great adventure than preparing me for mine. I hadn't gotten around to asking her where the name had come from. It had been all I could manage getting her to tell me how to flush the magical toilet in my apartment.

I mean, jiggling the handle as I sang, *Make me a Magic Muffin Mister*, wasn't just gross. It was also not at all intuitive.

I'm just sayin'.

Rather than trying to wrangle the information from the previous keeper, I silently promised myself that I'd change the name of the shop as soon as the paperwork was signed.

Best laid plans and all.

I'd tried to make the change. Multiple times. But the new sign I'd hung to replace the weather-worn wooden one bearing an ugly spotted frog and the name, *Croakies*, disappeared within hours and the old sign magically reappeared.

I'd tried burning the old sign once. It resurrected itself right back onto the front of my store.

I hadn't even been successful changing the name on paper. No matter how many times I filed a new name with the city. The old name simply reappeared on the paperwork in its place.

I gave up after the third try.

Croakies it was.

I had no idea why. But who was I to question the ways of the magical universe?

Sebille untangled her bony limbs and stood. "Do you want me to consult the mirror?"

I nodded. "Would you mind?"

She shrugged. "I'll be in the back room if you need me."

The "back room" of Croakies was the special area where all the magical artifacts lived. The front room was a bookstore. Though not your average bookstore. Even there, magic and supernormal reality dominated. But Croakies Books was available to everyone, which meant I got a lot of little old ladies looking for talking cat cozy mysteries and more than my share of ghost-busting wannabes.

As a city Sprite, Sebille made liberal use of the mirrors to gain access to magical news and happenings. Her family used streams and lakes and lived in toadstool houses. Sebille would disintegrate into a puddle of pique and rage if she had to live in a toadstool. That's why I'd dubbed her a city Sprite, though there really was no such thing. By contrast, her very large family found toadstool homes to be the height of comfort.

Part of my odd assistant's issue with the whole

"live in the woods in a toadstool" thing was that it required she maintain her traditional size of one and a half inches tall. Sebille had discovered she enjoyed being the size of the rest of the world, which enabled her to do all the stuff that was key to her existence. Such as drinking half-caff, mocha latte grande made with steamed almond milk and coconut sugar, and hanging out at the Vape bar with perfect strangers who told her everything about their lives and then wondered why they had.

Yeah, that was her other super power.

Sebille lived in a one-room apartment over the vapery across the street. She said she loved the atmosphere of the place and had even created her own vape flavor with magical herbs. I'd tried it once when she was in the testing stage and I'm pretty sure I entered a separate dimension for twenty very long minutes.

That was the last time I was going to be vaping with Sebille.

"Let me just wash out this mug and I'll be right down," I told her as she started down the steps leading to Croakies' back room.

Sebille flicked a hand dismissively and disappeared down the steps with thunderous steps. I'd never understand how someone whose natural state was teeny tiny with iridescent purple and green wings could be so heavy-footed.

Then again, it could have something to do with

the pointy red shoes. They hadn't had her size in the shiny monstrosities and Sebille had been "absolutely certain" she couldn't go on with her life if she didn't get them. She'd bought them anyway and stuffed the toes with cotton balls.

Thus the clomping aspect to her descent down my stairs. I'd personally witnessed the shoes taking a flyer more than once. I'd even been nearly clocked on the head by one once.

Shaking my head, I moved into the kitchen and ran water into the mug, adding some soap to the mix. Then I rinsed it out and placed it upside down in the drainer on my counter.

My head still ached, but it was much better than it had been before the tea. I splashed cold water onto my face and squinted around for a towel, finally remembering I'd put it into the laundry the night before.

Reaching blindly for the paper towels, I encountered an empty roll.

In desperation, I tugged my shirt up and dragged it over my face, leaving a large wet spot on the bottom.

Whatever.

I headed down to the first floor, suddenly anxious to discover the source of my magical headache. The sooner we figured out which artifact needed rescuing, the sooner I could get pain-free.

The door leading to the bookstore was at the

bottom of the stairs. I stopped and peered through the glass, seeing an empty store and a *Closed* sign on the door. Just as Sebille had said.

I released breath I hadn't known I'd been holding. It had been a long day and, though I loved my job at the bookstore, I was relieved that my day job wouldn't be interfering with my night job. for once

I locked the interior door and turned toward the large, open room behind the stairs. As usual, the light in the place flickered over the artifacts, a rainbow of colors that shifted and shuddered, depending on which artifacts held sway at the moment.

There was a light switch I could use to disrupt the natural light of the artifacts, but I'd never used it. I'd never felt the need to disrupt the artifacts' natural energy. I liked that they lit the space around them with an energy all their own.

I found Sebille standing in front of an ancient, wood-framed standing mirror, hands on hips and shoulders stiff. I recognized the tiny figure who stared back at her from the age-marbled glass.

"Don't be such a derk!" Sebille's mother exclaimed in a voice amplified by magic. It was very strange to see the bug-sized woman's lips moving and to hear a voice as big as her full-sized daughter's. "You know we must do as the magic commands."

Sebille leaned closer, her frame rigid. I couldn't see her freckled face but I could picture it in my mind. In her rage, the Sprite's features would be sharp, her skin giving off an iridescent glow that changed color depending on how mad she was. I was relieved to see it was only a mild pink, which meant she was irritated, but she wasn't going to be tempted to send an atom-shattering blast of magic into the treasure mirror in her present mood.

"Sebille?" I said as I approached. I spoke more to distract her from getting any angrier than for any other reason. I gave her mother a smile and a finger wave. "Your Majesty."

The Sprite's wings fluttered with pleasure and her tiny form dipped on the air before surging back up to eye level in the mirror. "Hello, Naida. How is your headache?"

I wrapped an arm around Sebille. "Better, thanks to your daughter's superhero level tea making abilities."

The Sprite in the mirror smiled regally. "I am glad. I hope you can help him, Keeper. I really do. Now I have to go." She shot straight up, out of view. The pond in the background sparkled for a beat before beginning to waver and then disappeared behind a silvery cloud of nothingness.

"He?" I asked my assistant.

Sebille dropped angrily onto a chair, her expression murderous. "Don't ask." She yelped and shot straight into the air, grabbing her buttocks and turning to glare at the chair. The red velvet and gilded wood furniture shifted back and forth as if wagging its tail and then settled into inactivity again.

I was pretty sure the gilded arms sparkled for a moment before returning to normal. "Casanova's chair," I told her, a laugh burbling in my throat.

"I'm aware of that, Naida!" She snapped, rubbing her bottom and glaring at the chair. "We should put that thing in the closet."

I allowed my laugh to escape, shaking my head. "I have. Five times. It just keeps showing back up at the front of the shop."

She sighed. "Sometimes, I hate magical artifacts."

I gave her a wink. "Yeah, but magical artifacts luuurrrvvve you!"

She somehow missed the humor in my teasing. "In the questionable vernacular of my Sprite mother, don't be such a derk, Naida!"

Shaking my head, I pointed to the mirror. "Did your mother have any insights for us?"

"Nothing very useful. She said the magical wave was mixed and vague. All she got from it was that it concerned a man." She pinched bony shoulders toward her pointed ears. "Maybe one of the artifacts in the shop has gone rogue."

I glanced around at the seemingly jumbled mess of things which looked harmless and innocent but which definitely weren't either of those things. Nothing glowed or shimmied or just generally looked agitated. "If so, I'm not sensing it here. Are you?"

Sebille opened her mouth to reply but didn't get the chance.

From the back of the room came a loud thump. I hurried in that direction, Sebille hot on my heels. No further sounds occurred to help us pinpoint the problem. After hurrying down aisle after aisle of dusty objects that didn't seem to be out of place, we came to the end of the last aisle and found the source of the problem.

Actually, he was the source of many of my problems. But he was just so dang cute!

I jerked to a stop and cocked my head, glaring down into a pair of round, orange eyes.

"Mr. Wicked!" Sebille uttered in her most irritated tone. "What have you done?"

The cat narrowed its startling eyes, which were actually a really dark gold but they often looked orange in the low light. He skimmed a glance in my direction and gave me a long, broken "Meow," then looked down at the thick, dusty tome his bottom was resting upon.

"What are you doing in here, Mister?" I asked the gray kitten as I scooped him up and placed a kiss on top of his head. His purr rumbled against my chest as I snuggled him close.

Sebille bent down to pick up the ancient, leather-bound text the cat had apparently knocked to the ground. "This book is two hundred years old, Naida," she whined, her long fingers wrapping around the spine. "It's delicate..."

The book skimmed sideways, banging against my foot. I looked at Wicked and he seemed to smile, even as his gaze narrowed with innocence. "What are you up to, cat?"

He shoved his back paws into my belly and I released him, watching him drop gracefully to the ground. He twined around my legs a couple of times and then looked up, giving me another throaty "Meow!"

Sebille put hands on hips, expelling an angry sigh. "Blast you back to the hellish environs you came from, you wicked feli..."

I slammed a hand over her mouth. "Don't you dare!"

Sebille glared at me over my hand, and then slowly tugged my appendage from her face. "I'm going home."

My first instinct was to agree, but then I remembered the magic wave. "But we haven't found the magical artifact that needs protecting." Even to me, my voice sounded a bit whiny. I couldn't help it. Sebille and I were like oil and water, but without her help I was totally in the dark.

A truly frustrating experience which made me feel inadequate on a daily basis.

She tossed a hand over her shoulder and kept

walking. "You'll be fine. Let that damnable cat help you find it."

She slammed the door between the front room and the artifact library and I fought to keep from stamping my foot.

"Meow!"

I glanced down to find Mr. Wicked sitting beside the book, whacking it with one of his paws as if trying to kill a bug. "Here, young man. Don't destroy the magical items." I grabbed the thick book and lifted it, brushing grime from the floor off its leather cover.

To my horror, the cover seemed to roll underneath my fingers, as if basking in the rubbing action of my touch. I almost dropped it, barely keeping hold with the tips of two fingers as it finally stopped moving. "Ugh!" I shook my head at Wicked. He was watching me as if he expected me to do something interesting.

I opened the book and flipped through its gold-edged pages, noting the yellowed but surprisingly well-maintained condition.

The pages were entirely blank.

I frowned. "Why in the world?"

The front door slammed and I jumped, sighing. Setting the book back into its spot on the shelves, characterized by a rectangular, dust-free area midway up from the floor, I headed toward the front room. "Come on, Mr. Wicked. We need to close the shop. Miss Huffy left without locking the doors."

Wicked hung back for a moment. But, by the time I reached the door into the bookstore, he was bouncing along beside me, short gray tail stuck straight up behind him. The kitten loved the stacks of books inside my magical bookstore and he never missed an opportunity to explore beneath the rows of shelves and in the corners for scraps of paper, bits of fluff, or forgotten string.

2

A RIBBITING EXPERIENCE

*W*icked trotted past me and ducked through the door when it was only open a crack, acting as if he thought I'd try to keep him from entering with me.

I shook my head. "Take it easy there, little man. You almost knocked me off my feet."

To all outward appearances, the determined cat couldn't have cared less. He'd already disappeared beneath the nearest shelf and seemed to be trying to scratch trails into the threadbare carpet. "Hey!" I called out to him. "Stop that."

The scratching stopped and I moved toward the front door, quickly turning the series of deadbolts and running my fingers over the air around the locks to make sure the warding was still in place.

The deadbolts were to keep human types from entering the shop when it was closed. Triggered when the physical locks were engaged, the warding would do the same job against the magical community.

Checking the ward was habit. I'd purchased it from a fourth-generation witch when I'd moved into the building and she assured me it would last until someone with power equal to hers came along to dismantle it.

Since her family was the oldest family of witches in Enchanted, I figured the chances of that happening were slim.

I closed my eyes as my fingertips felt their way along the familiar weave of the ward, feeling the distinctive threads, bumps, and dips of it against my skin. When I got to the end and felt the flashy Q for Quilleran which served as the lock for the magical ward, I smiled.

The warding was still good.

I turned away, heading to the counter where a messy pile of the day's receipts waited to be filed, and thought about the Quilleran clan. They were a strange bunch, secretive and borderline unfriendly with anyone outside the family. And they had an odd affection for cats. Particularly cats with magical sensitivities. Madeline Quilleran was estranged from her family, which rumor had it was mixed up in more dark magic than they should be.

One of the most powerful witches in the area, Madeline had warned me that her ward would keep her family out as long as I tended it. But if I let the threads weaken, over time, her brother Jacob would find a way to break it.

Needless to say, I didn't let the threads weaken.

Not all of the Quilleran witches were sketchy. I'd gotten Wicked from the youngest Quilleran, Maude, who'd appreciated my helping her locate an errant magical hairbrush she'd misplaced at Enchanted High, and decided to pay me back by gifting me a kitten from their latest litter.

I hadn't wanted to take the gift, knowing that owing a favor to a Quilleran was not a good idea. I'd insisted she offer me the kitten as payment for services rendered.

I was really glad I had too. Because it had made it so much easier to repel the girl's sisters as each and every one of them appeared on my doorstep trying to take the kitten back.

I might have given in to their nearly endless pressure that first few months if Mr. Wicked hadn't gotten such a look of pure terror on his beautiful little face every time a Quilleran walked through my door.

A steady thumping sound emerged from beneath the shelf where Wicked had disappeared. I glanced up from my filing to eye the space. "Mr. Wicked, what are you doing under there?"

Silence met my question, followed by the quick swipe of a gray tail across the floor at the edge of the shelf. "Whatever it is, stop it!" I told him, smiling at the knowledge that I was speaking to a cat who had no clue what I was saying and wouldn't care a whit if he did.

As if to prove my point, more thumping sounds emerged.

I dropped the pile of receipts and headed over there, sighing wearily. "Buddy, I can't afford to replace this carpet so I can't have you shredding it." I dropped to my knees and laid my head on the floor so I could see beneath the shelf.

At first, I saw nothing but shadows. No movement, no round orange eyes, no haughty snap of a gray tail that told me Wicked resented my micromanaging his life. I'd certainly seen that often enough.

"Mr. Wicked?" Something emerged from the shadows. The shape didn't move like a cat. It wasn't graceful. In fact, it sort of shuffled rather than walked. I suddenly feared that my sweet kitten had hurt himself. "Are you okay, buddy?"

The shape reached the light and I found myself staring into a pair of bulging black eyes, surrounded by a scaly green head and a fat, squishy body.

I yelped, jumping back in surprise as the frog leaped into the air and thumped against the underside of the shelf.

"A frog!" I squealed, backpedaling as fast as I

could on my knees until I bumped up against the base of the counter.

More thumping ensued. Then Wicked's head emerged and he glowered at me. "Meow!"

I felt strangely compelled to defend myself. "What do you want me to do?"

The cat yowled unhappily, disappearing back underneath the shelf with a final snap of his tail.

Thump. Thump. Thump.

I sighed. The frog was clearly stuck under the shelving. Every time he tried to hop out from under there, he bashed against the underside of the shelf. "I just..." I scrubbed a hand over my face, wondering who I could call to extricate him.

"Yowwww!"

"Sprite's trousers, Wicked!" I exclaimed in frustration. "I don't touch frogs. You know this. We've discussed it at length." Not that he'd understood any of it. But he seemed determined to force me into touching this one so I felt the need to remind him. "They're slimy and give me hives."

I wasn't sure that latter was strictly true. But panic was making my pulse race and I had to tell myself something.

Thump. Thump.

The poor thing was going to give itself brain damage. Wait. What was I saying? Frogs don't have brains. Do they?

Thumpthumpthumpthumpthump.

"Ugh!" I exclaimed, "I'm coming!"

I repositioned myself on the floor, glancing along the line of shelves. Maybe I could just cut the shelf down the middle so he could hop out.

"Meow!!!"

Growling unhappily. I pressed my cheek against the carpet and looked underneath again. The bulging black eyes seemed to be closer to the edge. *Maybe he'd managed to move himself*, I thought excitedly. Maybe he didn't need me after all.

The black eyes slowly blinked and the frog's body quivered. He looked so sad. I stared into those protruding eyes and something inside me shifted. I felt...pity.

"Trolls boogers," I murmured unhappily, knowing what I had to do.

I pulled air into my lungs and tugged a wisp of calming magic forward, unsure I'd be able to do it. My hand inched closer and stopped as the black, unfathomable gaze pinned me in place. The frog's body swelled and shrank as it breathed, and its tiny feet shifted uncertainly as my hand came close.

My fingers twitched. My hand stilled in midair. All I could think about was the last and only time I'd touched a frog. It had been cool and slimy to the touch, and its slime had painted my hand, giving me an unsightly rash that had lasted for weeks.

Nothing I'd done had helped the rash. Until I'd accidentally gotten blasted by a ray of healing magic.

I couldn't count on a random witch shooting healing magics at me a second time. Or, considering my unhealthy relationship with the Quillerans, a non-random one either.

Thumpthumpthumpthumpthumpthump...Meow!

I sighed, dropping my head to the floor in defeat. "Okay, chillax you two. I'm doing this."

Before I could change my mind, I quickly extended my hand and wrapped my fingers around the thick, squishy body, jerking it toward me and then releasing it with a squeal and another awkward crawling retreat.

The frog hunched on the carpet, staring at me with its throat working, its puffy body looking iridescent under the overhead lights. I rubbed my hand against my jeans, grimacing, before realizing my hand wasn't slimy. Not at all. And the touch memory of the frog's soft, warmish skin still clung to it.

"Ribbit," the frog said. It gave an experimental hop in my direction and stopped as I twitched with disgust. "Ribbit."

Mr. Wicked suddenly appeared at my elbow. He gave me soft eyes and rubbed against my knee as I stared in horror at the frog. It had just occurred to me that my trauma wasn't over. I still had a frog in my bookstore.

"Now what am I going to do with you?" I murmured. I had no idea what frogs needed to live. I wasn't equipped to deal with amphibians. I was totally a dry land kind of girl. What did they eat? Did they need water to survive?

A spec of black buzzed past me and Wicked's paw shot up, swiping at the fly. The unfortunate insect dodged sideways to avoid the threatening paw, and flew directly into deadly frog territory.

Quick as a wink, the frog's tongue snapped out and snatched the fly right out of the air. He seemed to shudder as if even he was disgusted by the action.

"Well," I said, grimacing. "I guess the food thing's taken care of for the moment."

I shoved to my feet. "Tomorrow, I'll ask Sebille to take you to her family in the woods. You can live on their pond," I inexplicably explained to the frog and the cat.

With that decision made, I felt better. But just in case, I went into the bathroom and grabbed Wicked's water dish, filling it up and carrying it out to place in front of the frog. "If you need a drink or... you know...a bath or something."

"Ribbit."

"Yowl!" Wicked gave me stink eye.

I shrugged. "Hey, it was your bright idea to save him. I guess you're going to have to take this one for the team."

I headed for the door into the artifact library and the stairs, suddenly exhausted from my very long day. I wanted to drop into bed and sleep for ten hours. But first, a long, hot shower and excessive scrubbing of my hand were in order.

It wasn't until I closed and locked the door behind me and Mr. Wicked that I realized my headache had disappeared.

No rash and no headache. My day was finally looking up.

3

BLANK EXPRESSION

I wish I could say my night was restful. Unfortunately, it was anything but. It was chaotic and just plain weird.

I drank my chamomile tea as usual and took a hot shower before dropping gratefully onto my bed. A soft rain had begun sometime during the night and the drops pinged musically against the glass of my windows.

It was a recipe for a great night's sleep. A veritable promise of one. Except that, from the moment I closed my eyes, my mind started churning with pictures that made no sense. First there was the frog. Yeah, it's weird that he was in my head but he was. I figure it was because of all the questions in my mind about his sudden appearance in my shop. I mean, a frog?

And then there was Mr. Wicked. His odd attachment to the frog was even stranger than the fact that I had a bug-eyed amphibian in my bookstore. My mind conjured scenes of a frog hopping through the shallow water at the edge of a pond. Then a flash of light that made the bulgy black eyes widen in fright.

And then nothing.

Well, not nothing exactly. More like something that wasn't really...anything.

Sigh. I know I'm not making any sense. But that's because my dreams didn't make any sense — especially the part where the frog was sitting in my teacup, wearing a bowtie.

Yeah, really. I wouldn't joke about a thing like that. You see...

No. It's easier just to show you. Here's a replay of my dream.

"Hey you!"

I jerked upright in my bed, looking around frantically for the random voice in my bedroom that had woken me up. I saw nothing except the charcoal gray shadows of my darkened room and the silvery drops of rain sliding down the windows.

"Helloooo?" an annoying voice drawled out.

I jumped, shoving the covers off my legs and surging to my feet. My heart pounded a frantic staccato rhythm in my chest and my fingers curled in an effort to contain repelling magics. "Who's there?"

"Ima."

"Ima who?"

"*Ima sick of waiting for you to see me sitting here.*"

I blinked rapidly. See you? Then it occurred to me it might be a ghost. Did I have ghosts in my loft apartment? More importantly, did I even believe in them? "Show yourself." My eyes scanned the room, finding only furniture, a thin line of illumination from the streetlight outside painting my floor, and...

"*Down here! Jeez, are you blind?*"

My gaze jerked down toward the floor and I jumped sideways, exploring the area around my feet with rising panic. "Where? I can't see you." I frowned, "Are you a ghost?"

Laughter, deep and...well, deep. "*Not hardly.*"

I dropped to my knees and looked under the bed, finding nothing but hairballs and a few dusty suitcases.

Hairballs! I jerked upright again, my gaze finding the spot on the pillow where Mr. Wicked always slept. His sleek, gray form was draped there, legs stretched out from his body and soft underbelly gently rounded from all the treats he begged from the customers in the store.

"*Sometime today would be nice,*" the deep voice drawled again.

I stiffened, finally realizing where the voice was coming from, and turned my head slowly, my eyes at the same level as the top of my nightstand. Where my teacup still sat.

But it was no longer empty. The frog from my bookstore was sitting inside the cup. Its squishy body bulging

over the sides of the delicate china. And, yeah, he was
wearing a bright red bowtie with yellow polka dots.

Hey, I don't make this stuff up.

The frog fixed its protruding gaze on me and its lips
seemed to curl up in the corners. "Hey. How's it goin'?"

Just like that, my dream ended. I jerked upright,
chest heaving with fear as my gaze shot to the teacup
on my nightstand.

No frog.

I placed a hand on my chest and willed my
heartbeat to slow. Groaning softly, I hunched over,
burying my face in my hands. I felt as if I'd gone
nightclubbing with a Tasmanian devil and his entire
spin class. Glancing at the clock, I saw with shock
that it was after nine am. I'd overslept and still felt as
if I hadn't slept at all.

I shoved the covers back and climbed out of bed.
I needed coffee badly.

Picking up my cup, I peered inside, looking for
frog poop or...I don't know...fly leftovers in the
bottom. There was nothing but tea dregs lying there.

I narrowed my gaze at the dregs. Was that a face
in the residue? Shaking my head, I chastised myself
for being an idiot. My imagination was running
amok. I was dreaming about frogs and seeing handsome male faces in my tea leavings.

Wait? Who'd said the face was male? And handsome? "I need to start dating again," I murmured as I
shuffled toward my coffee maker.

I scoured the cup thoroughly as the coffee brewed, washing it three times with hot water and soap, just in case there had been frog butt inside. Then I all but gulped the first cup as soon as it was cool enough to drink. I savored the second cup as my stomach rumbled hungrily.

Foraging desperately for something to eat, I realized the cupboards were mostly bare. I tugged an ancient box of granola out of the cabinet and looked inside. Grimacing at the paltry serving left in the bottom of the box, I shoved it back into the cupboard. Maybe I'd send Sebille out for some bagels.

Yeah. That was just the ticket.

Feeling better with the thought, I went to get dressed for work.

"**D**id you put this here?" I asked Sebille a while later in the shop.

She cast a glance toward the aged leather book and shook her head. "No. I thought you had."

I ran my fingers over the golden letters of the title, feeling their smooth, raised contours. "Blank Expression." I frowned. "What a strange title. Do you think it's supposed to be a novel?"

"More like a bad joke," Sebille muttered crankily.

A careful flip through the book proved that the pages were still blank. "Weird."

Sebille set aside the dusting rag and eyed the book, leaning over the counter as I turned the pages. "I don't think this book's that old." She placed her hand over an empty page, palm down, and closed her eyes. "Thirteen hundreds. Maybe late twelve hundreds. No older than that."

I couldn't imagine someone doing a joke book in the thirteen hundreds. "A journal, maybe?" I ran my fingertips along the page, searching for anything that might indicate hidden text.

Sebille opened her eyes and shrugged. "Doubtful. This was in the magical artifacts library. It has to have magical properties. Maybe the text appears when it's needed."

"That doesn't seem very helpful. How in a Troll's flipflops are you supposed to know when to look at it?"

Sebille set the dusting spray down next to her rag. "I'm going to lunch. Do you want me to bring you something?"

"No, thanks. I'm still full from the two bagels I ate for breakfast."

She headed for the door,

"You're sure you didn't bring this book up here?" I asked again.

"I'm sure," she called over her shoulder.

A soft, warm body twined around my ankles. I

glanced down, smiling. "Hello, Mr. Wicked. Where have you been all morning?"

"Meow."

"Where did you hide your friend?" I asked my cat, my curiosity tempered by the realization that I really didn't want to know. Where frogs were concerned, out of sight was delightfully out of mind. Unfortunately, telling myself that didn't make it so. I was vaguely aware of a niggle of worry about the little green guy. I didn't really know what kept frogs alive, but I was pretty sure whatever it was, my bookstore didn't have it. I sighed as I realized I needed to locate the frog and come up with a plan for him, moving forward.

As I straightened, the bell over the front door jangled cheerfully. I pasted on a welcoming smile, which immediately died when I spotted my visitor.

Candice Quilleran was the oldest daughter of the Quilleran clan. She was also the least trustworthy, the least honest, the meanest, and the greediest. In fact, it appeared that Candice was determined to be the "est" of all things.

She sent a shifting gaze around the shop, her wide, yellow eyes scouring every nook, cranny, and corner of the store before settling on me. When she blinked, she reminded me of a mean-tempered bird, like a vulture.

When she saw me staring at her, Candice twisted

her thin lips upward in a parody of a smile. "Naida. How are you?"

I bit back my honest response, which would have gone something like, "I was doing better before you came through the door," and nodded. "I'm just fine. How about you, Candice?"

She shrugged her response, her gaze sliding along the baseboards and between the rows of book-laden shelves.

"Are you looking for anything in particular?" I asked the other woman.

She started toward me, her expression turning sly. "I was looking for something...unique. I wondered if you might have it."

Thinking the unique thing she was seeking most likely started with Mr. and ended with Wicked, I played dumb. "And what would that be, exactly?"

She seemed to be searching for a crafty way of asking what she and the rest of her family had already asked a hundred times. I was pretty sure she'd come up with it. After all, she was the est-est of her entire family. "Do you sell, um, animals?"

And there it was. She truly did deserve her est title. "Mr. Wicked is not for sale."

She pretended to look shocked. "Mr. Wicked? The cat? Oh, my, no. You misunderstand. I'm looking for a different animal. Actually, he's not exactly an animal. He's kind of a, well, reptile maybe?"

She seemed to be asking me what she was

looking for. Even if I could see inside her mind — shudder — and interpret what I read there, I had no desire to put any effort into helping her. In fact, my energies were more likely to be spent in making sure she was disappointed in her search. "I don't sell snakes either. Sorry."

"Maybe reptile is the wrong word..."

"Lizards? Nope. Don't sell those either."

"He's really more of a..."

I was losing patience with the game. "Can you describe this...animal?"

"He's about this big," she held her hands about five inches apart and cupped them. "And he's got bulgy black eyes..."

An uncomfortable feeling made little alarmed flutters in the vicinity of my heart. I tried to wipe all expression from my face as I listened to her struggle not to tell me what she knew she needed to tell me.

I decided to play with her a little. "Are we talking legs or wings?"

"Legs, I guess."

"Gills or lungs?"

She frowned. "I have no..."

"Feathers or hair?"

"I think he's bald..."

"Warm blood or cold?"

Candice slammed a fist onto my counter and I blinked, fighting a smile. "I'm looking for a frog. I know he's here. If you return him to me now, I won't accuse you of theft."

Of their own volition, my lips curved into a not-so-nice smile. "A frog? Well, why didn't you just say so. I believe he's in the woods behind the shop."

She looked cautiously optimistic. "Really?"

I nodded enthusiastically. "At the pond. You can't miss him. He's green and has bulging black eyes."

Candice realized I was messing with her and her expression turned murderous. "You give me that frog, Naida Griffith or I'll curse you all the way through the next five generations of your kin."

I let the smile bleed away, tugging the roiling energy in my belly forward and allowing it to escape through my gaze. She blinked rapidly as a bright, silver glow filled my eyes, flaring brighter as my anger built. "You can swear at my family and me all you want, Candice Quilleran. That won't make me give you something I don't have. It won't even make me give you something I *do* have. Now leave this shop before I do something we'll both regret."

Much to my surprise, she spun on her heel and stomped toward the door, stopping as she wrenched it open and turning back to me. "You'll rue the day, Sorceress."

I flapped a hand in her direction. "I'll leave the ruing to you, bird. Now fly away before you really start to annoy me."

She did. And she slammed the door behind her

hard enough to vibrate the walls in my little shop. But I wasn't worried about the slamming door.

What I was worried about was the fact that the empty book flicked itself open as the door crashed into its frame and pages started flipping rapidly until they came to a rest on a page somewhere near the middle of the big book.

And a picture of my visitor the frog stared out at me from its yellowed pages.

4

A BUMPY CUP OF TEA

*a*s soon as the bumpy backside of Candice Quilleran disappeared behind the slamming door, Mr. Wicked emerged from his favorite hidey-hole in the cabinet underneath the cash register.

"Meow!"

"It's safe, little man. The evil witch is gone." I reached down and picked him up, holding him against my chest as he purred happily.

He rubbed the top of his head under my chin and then struggled against my grip and leaped onto the countertop, where he took up residence on top of the book with the empty flipping pages.

I mean, empty and flipping pages, not empty flipping...you know what I mean.

I stepped out from behind the counter and moved across the store, taking a seat at the small round table I'd set up near the shelves for patrons who wanted to peruse the books in greater depth before buying or renting them. I'd made two stacks of books on the surface of the table and was cataloging them for future sale.

My cup of rosemary tea sat cooling in between the stacks, its fresh aroma sweetening the air as I opened the first book. The volume was a compendium of advanced spells for healing warts and a wide variety of skin diseases. Not my most compelling item for sale in the shop, but definitely useful. The book I was cataloging was actually the second volume on the subject, which I'd purchased because the first volume was so popular on loan.

I reached for my tea without glancing away from the grotesque pictures of skin abnormalities in the thick tome and my fingers wrapped around a cool squishiness rather than the glossy handle of my favorite cup.

"Ribbit!" the squishy squatter belched out as my fingers squeezed him.

I shrieked, jumping out of my chair and taking three stumbling steps away. "What in the world?"

Just like in my dream, the frog was ensconced in my teacup. Its front feet, paws, hands, or whatever were draped over the rim of the cup and its black gaze was locked onto me.

"Ribbit."

"You already said that," I grumbled none too

happily. "How did you get into my teacup?" Even as I asked the question, I knew it was a silly one. After all, if frogs were known for anything, it would be for hopping. Clearly, my unwelcome intruder had hopped up onto the table. The larger question was *why* was he in my teacup?

Surely, he didn't think it was a tiny, fragrant pond?

I know. Don't call you Shirley.

Mr. Wicked trotted over on silent paws and jumped up onto the chair I'd recently vacated. He leaped onto the table and touched his nose to the frog's...um...snout?

I grabbed him, jerking him away. "Don't touch him or we'll be using that nasty book on warts and rashes to heal your cute little face."

Both cat and frog glared at me, obviously painting me as a frogist or an amphibian bigot or something equally hideous. I felt the irrational need to defend myself. "What? I don't like frogs. Sue me."

The door opened with the jingling of the bell and I hurried over to greet my neighbor Leandra, who owned an herbalist shop next door. Because of the magical nature of both our businesses, we often shared customers and sometimes worked together to help a desperate client.

She was also my best friend and a truly gifted witch.

As usual, Leandra was dressed in a flowing dress

that brushed her ankles and danced frothily on the air as she moved. Her well-padded form moved through the door with an unnatural grace and her turquoise gaze shot unerringly toward my little cup of problems on the table. "Ah," she said, "So, that's it."

Relief filled me as I, perhaps deliberately, misunderstood her statement. "Oh thank the goddess, he's yours?"

Lea's laughter was musical and filled with actual humor. "Mine? Not a chance, dove. He belongs to the Quillerans." She tucked a wavy strand of light brown hair behind one ear. "He's got their magic signature all over him."

Despair turned my stomach sour. I sighed, my shoulders drooping. "I guess she wasn't lying."

"Who?" Lea asked, walking over and plucking my visitor out of the cup as if she handled frogs every day. I had a sudden moment of concern as I tried to remember if Lea had any jars filled with floating frog parts in her shop.

"Candace Quilleran. She blew into the store a few minutes ago demanding that I give him back."

Lea's face flushed with irritation. "And yet here he still is."

"What can I say, it goes against my better instincts to give that woman anything she wants."

Lea placed the frog onto the floor and Mr. Wicked jumped down to sprawl beside him, batting his paws playfully in the frog's general direction.

For his part, the frog pretty much ignored my cat. His black gaze seemed...erm...ribbeted on Lea and me.

Sorry. I couldn't resist.

"How did *you* get him?" Lea asked as she watched the frog watching us.

"He just showed up. But he seems to be Wicked's friend."

Lea crouched down, her skirts tumbling around her legs like waves against the sand, and scratched my cat's chubby belly. "Who's a good little Familiar?" she cooed.

Wicked playfully batted at her hand, claws sheathed.

Lea smiled. "He gets cuter every day."

I couldn't help agreeing with a grin. "He refused to come out of his hidey-hole when Candace was here."

Lea stood, her expression turning serious. "You mustn't ever let her take him, Naida. He won't be safe there."

I hated when Lea told me that. She'd done it regularly since Mr. Wicked had become my companion. Pretty much every time one of the Quillerans had showed up at my store.

"As you've repeatedly told me. And I believe you," I hastened to add. "But I'd like to know why he wouldn't be safe. What would they do to him?"

She shook her head. "Some things aren't meant to be discussed. That clan is famous for casting dark magic spells. Many an enemy has suffered because of their evil ways."

I sighed. However bad her premonitions were, the fact that she wouldn't share them with me made them even worse in my imagination.

Lea seemed to think the Quilleran clan was capable of unspeakable things.

She cocked her head, her gaze returning to the frog. "His aura is the color of flame," she said.

"What does that mean?" I asked, interested. Any information I could get on the slimy intruder would help me figure out why he was there. I was starting to suspect he'd been the source of the magic wave that had sent me to my bed with a blinding headache the evening before.

"It means he's got a purpose that hasn't yet been determined," she told me unhelpfully. She cocked her head. "Or he's suffering from gastritis." She frowned. "Do frogs get gastritis?"

I snorted. "You're asking me? I thought they were reptiles until I read a book entitled, *Caring for Your Amphibian*."

Lea's mouth opened and I held up a hand. "Don't ask me why I read that book. Let's just chalk it up to one of life's little mysteries."

Her mouth snapped shut and she straightened, casting another look over my unwelcome visitor. "Do you want me to take him?"

Boy did I! But I knew that if I didn't discover the mystery behind the frog's sudden appearance in my store, the dancing pickle forks would make a quick reappearance in my life.

"No. But thanks. I think he's an artifact I need to rescue. Or he's tied to one. I'm not sure exactly what he is. I don't have a lot of experience with live artifacts." I thought about that for a beat and then affixed a qualifier to the statement. "Unless you consider a butt-pinching chair from the world's greatest perv alive."

Lea waggled her brows. "Mind if I borrow that chair on Saturday? That might be the most action I've seen in a while."

The guffaw burst out of me. I hugged my friend, shaking my head. "Trust me. You don't want Casanova's chair in your house. It will strip all the other chairs and get them pregnant before you can say, *howdy hoo, what's with you?*"

L ong after Lea left, I closed my inventory book and sat back with a groan. My back was stiff, my rump was sore, and I didn't want to catalog anymore.

Sebille was in the artifact library, apparently talking to either her mother or her boyfriend on the mirror. I could hear her less-than-melodic voice even through the closed door. Mr. Wicked had draped himself over the stack of books as I worked. His pretty fire-colored eyes were closed and he was limp as a noodle, clearly asleep.

His friend, Mr. Slimy was safely ensconced in the box from the donut shop where Sebille had gotten our breakfast. I'd put a shallow bowl of water in the box, a clump of moss Lea had brought over for his bed, and a few half-dead flies Sebille had captured buzzing around the artifact library.

I grabbed a couple of the big reference books and carried them to their assigned spot on the Rental shelves. Sebille stepped into the bookstore as I was reaching for two more. "Hey. Was that your mom?" I asked.

She grimaced, coming over to help me file the books. "My brother. He's such a derf. He was calling to see if he could borrow Mr. Wicked for a haunting this weekend. I told him Wicked didn't do that kind of thing. But he thinks I'm just being a gnish about it."

Sprites, if you haven't figured out by now, have their own range of swear words that pretty much has nothing to do with real language. To me, it seemed like they just made them up as they went along. But I knew that wasn't the case, because they all seemed to understand the meanings behind the gibberish words. "Haunting?"

She stopped with a couple of three-inch-thick books pressed against her chest. She was wearing her bright locks straight and free, the strands separating at the sides of her head to allow her pointy ears to show. Her striped socks of the day were orange and yellow. A particularly unfortunate color against the deep purple of her knee-length dress. "Cats are closely aligned to the spiritual world. They're useful conduits for reaching spirits and can be used to force a ghost onto this plane."

"Why would you want to do that?" I asked, shocked.

She shrugged, her expression filled with disgust. "Because you're a derf and a gnish and you want to get back at your girlfriend for dumping your butt."

"Ahh." I reached for the last book on the table. "Mr. Wicked is not a party favor for your family, Sebille."

She rolled her eyes. "I'm well aware, Naida. That's why I told him no." She walked away shaking her head, her disgust firmly displaced from her brother onto me.

I reached for the next book without looking, and my fingers touched warm leather. Too warm. I stilled, looking down as the leathery cover rolled under my touch. I jerked my hand away and stepped back, recognizing the phantom book from the artifact library

I hadn't put that book on the table. Had I?

"Sebille?"

A book slammed to the floor behind the shelves and I jumped, my pulse spiking. "Sebille?"

A moment later she called out. "Sorry. Dropped it."

Movement caught at the corner of my eye and my gaze jerked to the book. The pages were flipping wildly, showing blank page after blank page, and then stopping on the now-familiar picture of Mr. Slimy. When I reached to touch the picture, the page flipped over to another blank sheet. It didn't stay blank for long. Like blood seeping through tissue from a wound, letters rose slowly from the page. As my horrified gaze locked onto the rising ink, I finally recognized two words, and my pressure spiked to new heights.

Help me.

5

TIME IS OF THE ESSENCE

I stood at the counter, staring into the donut box. Inside, comfortably ensconced on his mossy bed, Mr. Slimy stared back.

"Are you just going to stand there and glare at that frog all day?" Sebille asked as she pulled on her coat.

My gaze snapped up in surprise. I glanced at the tea-kettle-shaped clock above her head. "Is it five o'clock already?"

"I'll see you tomorrow," Sebille said, clearly disgusted with me. You might have noticed a pattern. Sebille spent a *lot* of time being disgusted with me.

"Bye," I murmured back. The jangling bell on the door reminded me that I had to be careful. Candace Quilleran had already swooped down on me once, trying to get her hands on the frog. I knew that was just the initial salvo into our new episode of Pet Wars.

She'd be back. And if she wanted the artifact as badly as she seemed to want it, she wouldn't come through the front door the next time.

A simple expulsion warding wouldn't keep her away indefinitely.

Realizing that it wasn't safe to leave him in the shop overnight, I made a quick decision. "All right, Mr. Slimy. You're coming upstairs with me."

"Ribbit!"

As I looked down on the bright, black gaze and rhythmically throbbing throat, I had a sudden memory of him chowing down on a hapless grasshopper earlier in the day and gagged.

No, wait, that wasn't the tender moment I'd been going for.

Sigh.

Ah well, I already had bats in my belfry. I might as well have a frog in my bedroom too.

I scooped up the box, locked up the shop and headed for the stairs. Mr. Wicked came running from the artifact library when I called out to him, a spiderweb coating his fuzzy nose and a spider leg sticking out of one side of his mouth.

"Erg! No wonder you two are bosom buddies," I told the cat and the frog.

Neither one deigned to respond to my observation.

Snots.

Settling my tea on the bedside table. I pulled a novel out of the top drawer. I smiled, my fingers caressing the glossy surface of the supernormal adventure that had been written by my favorite author. "At last we can be together," I told the book.

Mr. Wicked jumped soundlessly onto the bed and nestled himself into the cat-shaped dent in the center of my spare pillow.

The frog stared at me from his box next to the lamp. I stared back. "What?" When he didn't respond, I said, "Has anyone ever told you that you have a very judgmental face for a frog?"

"Ribbit."

"Yeah, that's what I thought." I turned on the lamp and settled myself comfortably against my pillows. As usual, the book drew me right in, carrying me through a fun adventure filled with witches, ghosts, vampires, and other such entertaining creatures.

The human population's ability to get nearly everything wrong about the supernormal world never failed to charm me.

The warm room, the soft drone of Mr. Wicked's purring, and a gentle rain pattering against the windows soon lulled me into sleepiness. My eyelids kept trying to close but I kept jerking awake, determined to finish the chapter before letting Morpheus wrap me in his chiseled embrace.

But it wasn't meant to be. Within moments I'd lost the battle and my eyes had fallen shut. I jerked awake at the sound of the book hitting the floor, and my eyes flew open.

I spotted movement out of the corner of my eye and my gaze snapped in that direction. A dense gray haze, vaguely man-shaped, swirled on the air above my bed. I yelped, skittering sideways so fast I slipped off the bed and crashed to the floor.

Wicked shot up on a surprised yowl, his tail snapping.

I jumped to my feet and stood staring at the swirling shape, watching it slowly morph into a long body and a pleasant-looking face. The eyes sharpened, their color brightening until they were more blue than gray, and the mouth opened in a soundless plea.

I shook my head. "I don't know what you want."

My shadow-intruder frowned, then turned to the nightstand and pointed. My gaze followed his and I blinked. Mr. Slimy was out of his donut box.

And he was sitting on the Book of Blank Pages.

If I hadn't realized before that the frog was at the core of the recent magic wave, it would have hit me hard in that moment. But somehow the book was involved too. I tried to remember if I'd ever seen the Book of Blank Pages before the frog appeared.

I didn't think I had. But I just wasn't sure. I got about a dozen new artifacts a week. Some of them I'd gone out into the world to gather and safely ensconce in my shop. Some came to me, unannounced and usually with problems attached.

I started to shake my head again, still at a loss. The frog hopped off the book and the cover flipped open, pages flicking past at an increasing rate. It finally stopped and I figured I'd be seeing a picture of the frog on the page. Frustration made my chest tight. I didn't know what the book...and now the shadow-man...were trying to tell me.

I opened my mouth to tell him that when I realized the picture on the page had changed.

It wasn't Mr. Slimy on that page at all. It was a picture of a clock tower, the clock's face large and white, the time set to eleven forty-five.

I glanced at the digital clock on my bedside table and saw that it was only eleven fifteen.

"I don't understa..."

Mr. Slimy hopped into the air and landed on the page, sinking into the picture in the blink of an eye. I squealed in alarm, taking a step toward the page as Mr. Wicked ran toward the book with a yowl and leaped into the air.

"No, Wicked!" I shouted, but it was too late. My

adorable little gray fluff hit the page and sank into the picture right behind Mr. Slimy.

I gave a little scream and reached for the page. Then stopped as a wave of magic lifted toward me, my hand hovering over the page.

I turned slowly toward shadow man and saw him nod before the shadows condensed, whirled, and shot toward the photo in the book.

It hit me with the force of a second wave, agony spearing through my brain. I staggered forward, barely catching myself before I collapsed to the floor.

Too late, I realized I'd placed my hand onto the clock tower on the page.

A heartbeat later, the magic grabbed me at the top and the bottom and twisted, wringing me like a wet rag, and ripped me out of my bedroom and into a totally different world.

My feet slammed down on hard, uneven ground and slipped sideways. I fought to regain my balance, seeing the slippery cobblestones beneath my bare feet. High above my head, a slow, rhythmic ticking sound worked its way into my awareness. The sound was made deeper beneath a thick, roiling fog that filled the air until it was hard to see anything past five feet or so.

I looked up at the clock face, seeing the second hand ticking slowly toward the twelve.

Beneath the ticking, which entangled itself into

my heartbeats until I couldn't separate the two, another sound emerged.

The sound of footsteps on the greasy cobblestones.

My gaze swept toward the sound, narrowing in an attempt to see through the cloaking fog, and I saw the familiar, man-shaped form.

At his feet was another form, even more familiar. "Mr. Wicked!" I hurried forward, scooping my cat into my arms as he bounded toward me. I buried my face in his fur, feeling him all over as I snuggled him close to make sure he was unharmed.

He meowed, wriggling against my grip.

"He's fine."

I jumped as the shadow man spoke. As my eyes lifted to his, I was shocked to see that he was real. No longer a shadow. A tall, well-made man who looked to be a few years older than I was, in his late twenties, with a strong jaw, piercing blue gaze, thick black hair and the cutest pair of wire-rimmed spectacles sitting on his classically perfect nose.

There was something about his features that tugged at my memory. Something that twisted dread in my belly. But I couldn't place it in that moment. "Who are you?"

"That isn't important," he said in a husky drawl. "I need your help."

I frowned. "I don't know who you think I am, but..."

"You're the keeper of the artifacts," he said quite simply.

"Yes. But you're not an artifact."

"No," he agreed quite reasonably. "But I'm the victim of one. And I'm running out of time."

My gaze narrowed with distrust. "What exactly are you asking for?"

He lifted his arms out to the sides. "Isn't it obvious?"

"If it was obvious, I wouldn't be asking," I responded, growing impatient.

He looked down at the ground as if struggling for calm. Finally, he glanced quickly up at the clock and then back to me. "There's a device, a tea infuser, which when used pulls the essence of a person from his or her body. This infuser has been in the hands of a single owner for centuries, considered safe due to the pure consciousness and motives of its owner."

He hesitated and I jumped in, having heard the story way too many times in way too many variations. "Let me guess. It fell into the wrong hands?"

He nodded, lifting his arms again as if to say, ta-da!

"Wait, are you saying you have the infuser? *You're* the wrong hands?"

"What? No. Pay attention."

The tone, the snarkiness, the lack of patience all melded together to push a memory forward. It was the memory of a dream...and a frog with its nasty butt in my teacup. Then I realized what he was telling me. "You're Mr. Slimy?"

He sighed. "Such a terrible name. What were you thinking?"

"I was thinking it was a slimy old frog." I frowned. "What else would I be thinking."

"Frogs aren't slimy."

"I beg to differ. People have been getting high off frog grease for centuries."

"First of all, ew! And secondly, you're talking about toads, not frogs. There is a difference you know."

"Not in my mind. You're both bulgy-eyed and reptilian." I held up a hand as he opened his mouth to argue. "Don't bother telling me frogs are amphibians, not reptiles. You say potato. I say slimy reptile."

He shook his head. "If I'd known what a hardheaded, bigoted person you were..."

"You'd what?" I asked, clutching Mr. Wicked closer as he tried to escape. "Go to another keeper of the artifacts? I hate to disappoint but I'm it, honey. I'm all there is."

His lips curled and the recognition I'd been searching for slipped into place. I gasped. "You're a Quilleran!"

The clock started striking midnight as he lifted his hands in supplication. "Please! I only have until the waning moon to be returned to my body or this is permanent."

His face paled as the fog started to swirl around me, agitated and thickening fast as the hour struck down. My legs disappeared into the fog from my feet to my knees and it quickly climbed upward.

He took a step forward. "No, wait! Please!"

But I had no control over whether I stayed or left. And I was pretty sure I wouldn't have stayed anyway.

Troll boogers! He was a Quilleran. And I'd let him into my home, into my bedroom. Sure, he'd been ensconced in a grease-coated donut box...but still.

The magic wrapped clutching fingers around Wicked and me, twisting us in a relentless grip that felt, for a terrifying beat, as if it would rip us into pieces, and then flung us through the shadowy fog, where my mind, thankfully, stopped registering the pain or the dizzying spin of power around me, and eased me into a charcoal nothingness.

6

SHIRLEY YOU JEST

I awoke to a blindingly bright sun peering through my window the next morning and sat bolt upright, looking around in surprise to find myself in my own bed again, on top of the covers and sideways as if a giant hand had flung me onto the bed.

Wicked!

My gaze flew to the top of the bed, and the terror leached from my chest when I saw him curled into his favorite spot on the pillow. His eyes opened as if he'd felt me staring and he stretched, yawning widely.

I flopped back onto the mattress. "Thank the goddess."

Then I remembered the frog and I jerked upright again. I lunged at the donut box, unsure what I was going to do, but certain at the very least that I was going to get the fat little traitor out of my bedroom.

He was gone.

Had the Quillerans already snatched him back? Maybe they'd known he was in the clock tower place and had yanked him from there.

I dropped the box back onto my nightstand and told myself I didn't care. He'd lied to me, though not really, and tried to fool me into helping him.

But if he was a Quilleran, why had Candace been so menacing about getting him back? She hadn't acted like she was doing it out of love.

Were Quilleran's even capable of love? Surely not.

Yes, I'm talking to you, Shirley.

The air sparkled above the box and I leaned away from it, seating myself on the edge of the bed and waiting.

A burst of light made me blink and a tiny form hung in the air in front of me, enormous moth-like wings undulating on the air like an airborne manta ray.

The tiny, puckish face frowned in my direction. The famous Shirley of "don't call me Shirley" stared down at me, her customary glare fixed on her face. Shirley was a pixie. She was also the supernormal world's version of Witch-a-pedia, with fun trivia and occasionally useful information about all the magical families and their ancestors. Inexplicably,

Shirley hated being a Witch-a-pedia. Which was why she never wanted anyone to call her.

And you thought that was just a cute saying, didn't you?

"Hey, Shirley."

She placed tiny hands on teeny hips and glared at me. "I told you not to call me that."

"I need to know if Quillerans are capable of love."

She pounded the air with her drab brown wings and rose above my head for a beat, still glaring. When she finally spoke, it was as if she had to wrench every word from her breast. "Quillerans can love but it is rare. Most of the clan love only power and control."

"So, they're politicians, then?"

Shirley tossed her head, which was covered in tight, dirty-blonde pin curls, and arched a pair of very judgmental eyebrows. "Don't call me again." She glared toward my kitchen table. "By the way, you have a frog in your teacup." Then she disappeared in a burst of light that left behind a slight sulfur stench, like the scent left behind when a matchstick expires.

I looked at Slimy.

He looked back at me. "Ribbit."

I sighed. "Okay, so they didn't take you. But why do they want you back so badly?"

"Ribbit."

"Very helpful." I thought about it for a moment. "I'm pretty sure that Candace isn't trying to get you back because of a deep and abiding love for you," I mumbled to myself. "And if they stuffed you into a frog like you said, there'd be no reason for them to care about you now. I'll have to assume you've gone rogue and they're trying to stop you from doing...whatever."

I narrowed my gaze at the frog. His gaze didn't narrow. "What are you up to, Slimy My Man?"

The downstairs bell jangled, yanking me from my thoughts.

Sebille had arrived to open the store. I shoved the previous night's adventure aside and went to fix some coffee to jumpstart my day.

I'd make time later to research the tea infuser issue. If he'd been telling me the truth about that, the consequences could be dire indeed.

I needed to get hold of that infuser before somebody did something really horrible and changed the world for the worst.

If I wasn't already too late.

I left Sebille in charge of the shop while I perused the books on ancient artifacts that I carried in the bookstore. When I'd gone through all of the available texts and found nothing,

I resorted to the stacks of books I'd relegated to the artifact library.

With Mr. Wicked trotting at my heels, I walked through the warehouse-sized space as magical lights flickered on far above my head.

First-time visitors to the artifact library were always shocked by the magically enhanced space, which from the outside appeared a fraction of the size it actually was.

The room was filled to the brim with magical artifacts of all kinds, sizes, and shapes, from a motorcycle that could fly, to a pair of socks that helped its wearer travel between dimensions.

High above my head, long, narrow windows allowed sunlight to filter into the space while keeping curious gazes from seeing inside.

A magical ceiling fan, its blades longer than I was, spun lazily from the apex of the domed ceiling, purifying the air as it kept the temperatures constant.

I sat down at the scarred wooden table located in the written artifact section of the room, a stack of books nestled in my arms. With a weary sigh, I pulled the first book off the top and placed it in front of me. The black leather cover bore a line of bold hieroglyphs in red, the ink it was printed with still bright after thousands of years. The edges of the book were slightly ragged, the leather scruffy with age, but the pages inside had been magically preserved under a gloss of shimmering energy and looked as good as the day they were created.

I slid a pair of wire-rimmed glasses onto my nose, taking a deep breath before starting to read the glyphs adorning the creamy yellow pages.

With the glasses, which were discovered by British archaeologist and Egyptologist Howard Carter in 1937, shortly before his death, I could read and understand any language I encountered.

There was only one, small side effect from the glasses, after I took them off, every word I tried to read for about an hour following their use looked like gibberish.

Sebille found me there after a couple of hours and settled a steaming cup of tea in front of me. The floral scent tugged at me as I pulled off the glasses and closed a slim volume of "The Magical History of Tea Making", pushing it aside. I'd found nothing useful regarding a tea infuser artifact in any of the books.

"No luck?" Sebille asked, dropping her fanny onto the edge of the table and crossing her arms.

I sipped, sitting back with a sigh. "Nothing. I'm starting to think Mr. Slimy lied to me."

Sebille frowned thoughtfully. "I don't remember anything in the legends attributing any kind of special power to tea infusers. I could ask my mom."

I nodded. "Maybe it isn't an ancient device. Maybe someone magicked it more recently."

Sebille shook her head. "It seems unlikely. A spell to remove someone's essence is incredibly powerful magic. I'm not sure there have been any magic users since the Medieval days who could create something that dark and powerful."

"Not even the Quillerans?"

She took a moment to consider my question before responding. Finally, she shook her head. "Doubtful. But I suppose if they'd found a way to merge all their energies..." Her eyes went wide. "Mr. Wicked."

I blinked in surprise. "What about him?"

"I've heard rumors about his litter. Apparently, they were the result of a pairing of the two most powerful witch familiars. There were rumors in Toadstool City that the Quillerans had a specific purpose for the kittens." She lifted a bright red brow. "All of them."

Understanding blossomed. "Then, when Maude Quilleran gave Mr. Wicked to me..."

"She intruded on their plans." Sebille nodded.

"But apparently the magic was successful. If what Mr. Slimy tells me is true, anyway."

"Yes." Sebille stood up. "I'm going to talk to my mother." She headed toward the back of the room.

"Wait, aren't you going to use the mirror?"

She kept walking. "No. I think I need to go to the forest for this one."

I surged to my feet. "I'm coming with you."

To the normal human type creature, the forest where the Sprite Queen and her people lived probably just looked like any other woods, with regular-looking trees arching over moist ground that was covered in wildflowers and low-lying weeds and vegetation.

To me, the Enchanted Forest earned its name and then some.

The woods were dense with trees. Towering high into a cloudless blue sky with thick arms covered in rich hues of green. The trunks of the ancient trees were bigger around than I was, some of them twice or double my size. Carefully cultivated flowers in all sizes, colors and shapes dug their roots into the rich black soil around the massive trees' far-flung feet.

The wonderful mix of smells ran the gamut from the earthiness of the fertile soil to the variety of natural perfumes wafting all around us on a soft, warm breeze.

Unlike what a human might experience in the wood, it was far from quiet. My ears were bombarded with a cacophony of sounds and voices. From the belching song of the fat bullfrogs along the wide creek, to the happy chirp of a thousand different insects, and the shrill tones of a thousand Sprites, Fairies and Elves that populated the popular forest.

It wasn't quiet. But, to me at least, it was definitely peaceful.

It was the sound of a happy, vibrant colony of supernormal creatures who'd found their perfect spot to live in the world.

"At this time of day, she'll be in the palace," Sebille told me, grimacing. "You'll have to wait outside for me."

I shook my head. "Not a chance. I have questions for the queen. I need to speak with her."

My assistant's freckle-speckled face wrinkled with distaste. "I can't just command her to come out to see us. She is the Queen after all."

"I'm not asking you to do that. I have a chip left over from when I found her missing ladybug necklace."

Sebille looked only mildly mollified. She hadn't wanted me to take on the ladybug necklace job. It was still a source of disagreement between us. Even though it had ended moderately well.

I'd returned the Sprite Queen's favorite piece of jewelry to her, earning definite brownie points with the creature who ran the entire Enchanted Forest, but I'd had to burn a favor with another, more delicate connection in the process.

It was a win. But not a win-win. I'd made an educated decision that had ended with a measured outcome.

I was pretty sure I'd do it again if I had to.

I only hoped I'd never have to.

Sebille stopped at the edge of a magical place. I smiled as I did every time I saw the Queen's kingdom. Stretched out beneath the protective arms of the forest's largest tree, with the clear sparkling water of Magic Creek as its southern boundary, were hundreds of toadstools, nestled close and filling every inch of available space.

They were all different sizes and shapes, colors and patterns. Pretty green ones covered in delicate brown spots, oversized white ones with tawny underbellies, even tree-shaped toadstools whose surface reminded me of pictures of a brain I'd once seen in one of my magical reference texts.

There were pink ones with purple stripes, yellow ones with orange spots, stools with lacy underbellies that looked like an old-fashioned woman's skirt, and dispersed strategically among the rest, toadstools that were so vibrantly blue they mirrored the hues of the sky above. I'd learned from Sebille that those were specially magicked stools. They were warded to give warning on a variety of things, from dangerous weather, to approaching airborne predators, the inadvertent predators of the human or supernormal variety.

Too many Fae had been injured by humans walking through the wood without paying attention, carelessly stomping on a toadstool home before realizing what they'd done.

Not that they would have cared if they had. Since humans were blissfully unaware of the teeming life beneath their feet and before their very eyes.

"You have the chip?" Sebille asked.

I nodded, digging a tiny pebble from my pocket and handing it to Sebille.

She examined it carefully and then nodded, slipping it into a small box attached to the protective Redwood tree.

She closed her eyes and spun her finger in front of my face. Once, twice, three times, and then opened her hand, slamming her palm right at my face. I blinked in surprise but her hand stopped unerringly, a fraction of an inch from the tip of my nose.

Almost immediately I felt the burn of her magic sliding through me, starting at my toes and rising quickly up my legs, torso, hands and arms, neck and then head.

A deep, red flush followed the magic over my body, until all visible skin was the color of an over-ripe tomato.

The burn increased, causing me to grit my teeth against the pain. I had to fight to keep my protective magics from kicking in, knowing I'd only get one chance to accept the magic and, if I rejected it, my chip would be null and void.

Flower-scented air whispered over me and I opened my eyes as Sebille's form throbbed once, twice, and then disappeared from sight on the third pulse.

The ground beneath my feet rumbled violently. A quick jolt of fear brought my pulse spiking. I stumbled forward, trying to stay on my feet as the rumbling continued, growing in intensity.

A horrific bellowing noise had me spinning around, a cry on my lips as a gigantic, furry creature with huge ears and massive teeth thundered toward me.

I stood transfixed, watching my imminent death approach.

A hand snaked out and wrapped around my wrist, yanking me sideways as the enormous bunny landed right where I'd been standing.

I turned to find Sebille glaring at me. "Do you have a death wish?"

Confused, I glanced down at myself. I looked the same. But when I turned my gaze on Toadstool City, I gasped.

The stools were the size of human buildings. I could see the streets, filled with hundreds of walking, flying and gliding Fae.

The air beneath the closely-spaced stools buzzed with flying Sprites, their wings fluttering with iridescent vibrancy in the lacy sunlight that managed to filter past the tree branches far above. The Sprites moved from one place to another in the city with determined expressions, their hands generally filled with bundles of goods, or packets of papers to be delivered to the palace.

The Sprites were the government in Queen Sindra's kingdom. Every single Sprite had a government job. I knew that was the biggest bone of contention between Sebille and the queen. When my assistant had left Toadstool City behind, she'd left more than a home and friends.

She'd left an important position at the Queen's side. Her responsibility as a key advisor. And that was just never done.

"Come on. Let's get this over with. I don't want to be here past nightfall," Sebille murmured crankily.

When night fell, the city would go into lockdown. Magical aversion warding would be coupled with protective spider webbing to keep everyone who lived there safely inside the city, and those who didn't belong firmly outside the protections.

I nodded, falling quickly into step beside Sebille. I didn't want to be trapped through the night any more than she did.

Queen Sindra's palace was at the very center of Toadstool City. It rose above the other stools both in size and vitality of color. With a massive, domed roof painted a vibrant purple and covered with bright yellow splotches, the palace formed the perfect center point, a lively array of stool-lined spokes that represented the city's streets radiating from it.

All roads in Toadstool led directly to the palace.

When we approached the rounded yellow door of the entrance, two Elves dressed in the solid black attire of the Queen's guards moved from the sides to block us.

They wore large, golden seals on golden chains around their necks. It was the only adornment on the severe black uniforms.

When they saw Sebille, they inclined their heads and stepped back. But that didn't stop them from giving me a wary glance as I moved past.

I bit my tongue on the desire to offer them an excuse for my being there, forcing myself to remember that the city ran on a hierarchy.

Explaining myself to the guards would be like explaining the transmission of malaria to a disease carrying mosquito. Neither would care what I was up to unless it meant trouble for them.

I followed Sebille into a small entryway whose only furnishings were dense banks of sweet-smelling flowers.

Sebille strode past several Sprites with little more greeting than a nod and I had to hurry to keep up with her.

The place was built like a honeycomb, consisting of hundreds of small, octagonally-shaped rooms that served as buffers and barriers to the central space where the Queen lived. Each chamber in the honeycomb held at least one guard, sometimes two, and each time the guards started to confront us, only to back away once they saw Sebille.

I'd only been to the honeycomb palace one other time and I hadn't been with Sebille that time. I'd been accompanied by one of Sindra's guards because she'd requested my presence in her rooms.

Seeing the deferential treatment Sebille was being given, I wondered for the first time why she chose to remain my assistant at Croakies rather than taking her rightful place with her people.

There had to be a story there and I needed to find out what it was.

Glancing at Sebille's tense expression and tight jaw, I realized that information was not going to be coming my way anytime soon.

We finally emerged from the last honeycomb and stepped into a large, central space. Though the ceiling high above our heads was enclosed, the space wasn't as dark and dreary as I'd expected. In fact, the entire perimeter of the octagonal space was lined with layers of flowering plants and trees. The scent was light and wonderful, and patches of sunlight from octagonally shaped openings around the walls made a bright and pleasant space.

A constant buzzing sound filled the space. I eyed the flowers and noted the multitude of bees, busily buzzing from bloom to bloom as if they were driven by a single purpose.

I realized what that purpose was when I spotted

the honeycomb nests lining the walls of the entire space.

Somehow, Queen Sindra had become the Queen Bee of her own, massive hive.

I had known the Sprites made their own honey, and that it was cherished for both its medicinal as well as psychotropic qualities. But I hadn't realized how key to its making their queen was.

Queen Sindra watched us walk across the mossy floor covering toward her. She had no throne in the space. She rarely sat. If she wasn't standing, serenely overlooking the business of her kingdom, she was buzzing back and forth like her bees, her enormous pink, purple, and neon green wings pounding the air with gentle purpose.

She stood with her hands folded in front of her. Her wings pulsed gently behind her, ready to take flight at a moment's notice. But I didn't take the movement personally. She never rested until the cloaking magics fell into place at night.

Not even among her own people.

Sindra spared me a quick smile as we stopped before her. "Hello, Naida, dear. How are you?"

"I'm fine, Queen Sindra. Thank you for asking."

She nodded once, pleasantries concluded, and turned an unsure smile on Sebille. "Daughter. How do you fare?"

I saw the telltale tightening around Sebille's eyes that told me she was fighting an eye roll. Sebille hated the old ways of the Sprites. She hated the clinging to tradition Toadstool City represented, the archaic language spoken within the palace's walls. Even the palace itself because of the hierarchy it represented. "I'm fine. I just came to speak to you about the latest magic wave."

The queen's mouth tightened at Sebille's brusque manner. But she inclined her head, her expression turning business-like as she turned to me, excluding her daughter. "I've sent the Elves out to test the wave. They can't trace it to anyone in particular. But they did say there's definitely a strain of dark magic woven into it."

"The Quillerans?" I asked, frowning.

She pressed her palms together, fingers pointed upward as her wings juddered with displeasure. "We just don't know. But the strands contained bits of time manipulation and cell re-designation." She frowned. "I don't have to tell you that, with dark magic as the glue, it's a terrifying mix, Naida."

I frowned. "I figured as much."

"Have you identified the artifact?"

"I'm not sure." I told her about the frog and the book that came forward when he arrived.

She listened carefully, cocking her head like a curious bird. When I'd finished, she thought about what I'd told her before responding. "I've heard of live artifacts before. Though it's spectacularly rare." She didn't look as if she was convinced.

"What do you think about the clock tower?" I asked, trying not to show her how concerned I was. I didn't like the idea at all that whoever was behind the current artifact disruption could reach into my home when I was at my most vulnerable and drag me through time and space to a place I didn't know.

"Very disconcerting." She reached out and touched my hand, her skin cool and soft. "Naida, I'd like you to consider calling an Assembly on this one."

An Assembly was a massive gathering of all the supernormals in the area for the purpose of discussing a specific situation that might affect everyone. It was a loud, complex and long-drawn-out affair and it would yank the situation out of my hands and throw it up for determination by the group.

I experienced a jolt of instant rejection at the thought. "I'm not ready for that yet."

"The Quillerans would be part of the Assembly," Sebille told her mother, her expression grim. "I think that would be a mistake."

One of the guiding principles of an Assembly was that no supernormal could be excluded. Everyone had the right to have a say.

"Yes, that is a concern," Sindra agreed.

It always surprised me when Sindra took her daughter's advice without challenge. She was as proud as any queen I'd ever met, yet she trusted

Sebille in a way I'd rarely witnessed in a royal. It almost made me regret Sebille's decision to forgo her position as her mother's advisor. Though it would be a great hardship for me to lose her help at Croakies.

"But at some point you may not have an option," the queen told me. "I fear you're up against something more powerful than anything you've faced before."

Well, that just sucked.

I nodded, trying to keep my expression neutral. "You'll tell me if the Elves turn anything up?"

"I will."

"Have you ever heard of a spell or artifact that could pull the essence out of a person?"

Sindra shook her head. "That is the darkest of all magics, Naida. If there's a supernormal who's using that type of magic, we don't have precedence for how to deal with it." Her cool fingers tightened over mine again. "And I'm deeply troubled by the way this came to you, dear. You're an artifact keeper. You're not equipped to deal with magic as potentially dark as this. I'm not sure you have the training to handle it. The very fact that it came to you is very concerning."

"Why?" I asked, though I was pretty sure I already knew the answer.

"Because it doesn't truly belong to you. There's a good chance this isn't an artifact issue at all. It's a rogue magic user issue. And the fact that someone was able to manipulate the channels to have the assignment given to you..." She let the thought die on her lips, leaving me to determine the terrifying truth on my own.

Someone intentionally gave the wrangling assignment to me. Because, once I'd failed, the Assembly couldn't send another investigator out to find the culprit and deal with it.

Humans weren't the only ones who had a double jeopardy law on the books.

I probably wouldn't care anyway, in the end. Because the only way I was allowed to "fail" an assignment was to die.

7

AN ILL WIND JUST BLOWS

To say I was surprised to find a Quilleran at my door when I arrived back at Croakies would be a slight understatement. Not, mind you, that she was at my door, but that she was "at" my door and hadn't blasted through it or used a magical key to unlock it and let herself inside.

Quillerans generally didn't waste energy on mundane things like manners, rules or human law.

It wasn't Candace this time. It was her sister Felicity, whose dark brown hair and matching brown shirt and ankle-length brown skirt were perfect representations of her dour personality.

The only color on her entire person was in the muted yellow of her angry eyes.

"Well, hello there," I said to Felicity as I approached, waggling my brows suggestively just because I knew it would put her in a dither.

Her eyes went wide and she clutched her suitcase-sized bag protectively across her middle. "Naida. I wanted to talk to you."

I pushed past her, inserting my old-fashioned key into the lock and blocking her view as I turned it three times to the right and then a half-turn back to unlock the door.

I'd gotten the key when I purchased the rights to Croakies and had tried to chuck it, along with the locks, in favor of shiny new hardware for all my doors. But the locksmith, a practicing sorcerer who was dating my bestie Leandra at the time, had assured me the lock was the best in anti-theft magic available, so I'd decided to keep it.

I shoved the door open, grabbed a few pieces of mail off the carpet, and glanced over my shoulder. "What can I help you with?"

Felicity stood in the open doorway and glanced around the shop for a moment, her gaze wary. She stood on the threshold so long I was beginning to wonder if she was waiting for an invitation to come inside.

Like a vampire.

If so, she'd be waiting a while.

I ignored her as I settled my purse behind the counter and sorted through my mail.

After a moment, the soft scuff of a shoe on the worn carpet told me Felicity had thrown caution to the wind and come inside. I looked up to find her standing several feet from the door, her gaunt face tight with worry.

It was almost enough to make me feel sorry for her.

Nah.

"What did you want to talk to me about, Felicity?"

The woman looked down at the bag she was clutching close and, for the first time, I realized the bag was moving. I narrowed my gaze on it. "What do you have in there?" I tensed, pulling energy into my fingertips in case I needed to put the whammy on her or whatever she'd brought into my store.

I said a quick prayer to the goddess that it wasn't a snake. I couldn't abide snakes.

"I...I thought maybe we could do a trade."

I let the energy recede just enough that I wouldn't accidentally blast her with it when I came out from behind the counter. I wasn't trained as a warrior. I had only enough power in my core to turn her hair frizzy or make her pee herself. A useful tool for the beautiful but perennially mean girl in the cheer squad, but not much good when battling dark magic witchery.

I kept my distance just in case. Then I thought of Mr. Wicked. Had I left him in the artifact library? Or had he been in the bookstore when I'd left? I placed my hand on the counter and slid his cubby a surreptitious glance.

The door was open a crack and I didn't' see him inside. I breathed a quiet sigh of relief, the tightness in my belly receding.

My relief plunged into my colon as the surface beneath my fingers warmed and rolled.

I snatched my hand away from the Book of Blank Pages sitting on the countertop.

How had that gotten there?

Felicity's attention was drawn to the book. Something told me not to let her see it. I quickly leaned sideways, resting my forearm on the tome and fighting not to recoil when the surface bubbled beneath my skin.

The witch held my gaze for a moment and then slowly inserted a hand into the bag, her eyes locked on me the entire time.

I tugged my energy forward again, stepping away from the counter. I didn't bother trying to hide it that time, letting her see it spitting at my fingertips and glowing in my gaze. "What are you doing?"

She smiled and it wasn't a pleasant sight. "Why? Are you planning to curl my hair for me?" She snickered meanly. "I was only going to get this..." Her hand came out of the bag and she was holding a...bullfrog?

I blinked. "You brought me a frog? Why? Is this one of those psychedelic frogs that you're supposed to lick when you want your evening to be just a little bit more entertaining?"

"You're really weird, Naida."

I shrugged. She wasn't wrong.

"No. I thought, since you like the other frog so much, you might like this one even better."

"Why would I like it better?"

"It's bigger. And it croaks out the tune to *Night of the Fairies* on command."

"Night of the Fairies, huh?"

She nodded.

I waited a beat and then laughed. "You must think I'm really stupid."

"Of course. But I'm not lying. I can prove it to you."

I shook my head. "So, you can magic this poor frog to sing a song. That's a parlor trick. Why are you really here, Felicity?"

Her expression tightened with anger. A soft breeze rose up in the room and it blew her long brown skirt around her bird-like legs. The frog in her grip croaked in alarm and leaped out of her hands, hopping toward me and disappearing behind the counter.

"I want that frog, Naida."

Was it my imagination or had the witch's voice deepened a few octaves?

The breeze in the room turned into a gust, blowing the mail I'd just brought inside off the counter and onto the floor. Felicity's lank, brown hair blew away from her face, making her look like a powerful and extremely unattractive angel.

I backed up, my hand falling to the book on the counter. As I touched it, the cover flew open and the pages started to flip.

I grabbed it and tugged it off the countertop, shoving it onto the paper-strewn shelf underneath.

A deep, throaty song sounded at my feet. I yelped as the bullfrog hopped onto my shoe and squatted there, black eyes bulging with fear.

Okay, they'd been bulging before. But I was pretty sure I saw a glint of terror in their inky depths.

Felicity raised her arms and the wind strengthened. Books started flying off shelves and crashing to the floor, their pages ripping and pieces of the paper flying around the room.

I needed to do something, anything, to stop her from destroying my store.

But what?

I tried to think but my mind was in panic mode.

Beneath the counter, the pages of the book continued to flicker forward through the ancient volume and then back again as if searching for something.

"Give me the frog!" Felicity's voice boomed through the shop.

A freestanding shelf unit near the back wall lifted off the floor, the dozens of children's books it held flying into the air and slicing toward me, like missiles. I ducked as a book entitled, "The Care and Feeding of Your Invisible Friend" flew right at my head and smashed against the wall above the register.

"Stop it!" I screamed.

Felicity ignored me.

The signed picture of me, Lea, and the rest of our supernormal women's soccer team the year we won our league lifted off the screw holding it to the wall and shot toward me like a lance, glass first. My hand shot up in self-defense and I threw out enough energy to halt it an inch from my face, grabbing it out of the air and tucking it safely behind the counter.

"Felicity, just stop it!"

"Give me the frog."

I shook my head. "Not going to happen."

Another shelf lifted off the ground and I realized I had to do something or she was going to destroy the whole place.

I ran in her direction, intending to throttle her into stopping. But five feet away from Felicity, I hit a wall of wind that not only stopped me but slowly pushed me back. I dug in but couldn't get enough purchase on the floor to stop the backward motion.

Felicity flung her hands forward and the force of the gust tripled, flinging me backward until I crashed painfully into the wall.

Groaning, I fell to the carpet and crawled behind the counter.

The book had stopped flipping pages. I glanced at it, thinking I'd see another picture of the frog or even the clock tower. But it was neither.

A lightning bolt skimmed across the page.

Very helpful.

I glanced over the counter and my eyes widened. Something was happening behind Felicity. Something dark and shadowy surrounded her, seeming to wrap around her like a cloak. She turned pale, her eyes widening as the shadow covered her arms and they began to lower. The wind lessened. Felicity shrieked in rage and spun, her hands flying up like claws and wrapping around the shadow as if it had substance.

I watched in terror.

What in the...?

Felicity fought the shadow back, sending energy into it until it disappeared in a sulfurous gust of air. Then she turned back to me.

Her yellow gaze blazed with evil light, sparks literally shooting from her eyes. Ice filled my belly and crept along my spine.

The woman was seriously scary. And she looked like she wanted to kill. Me.

I started to back toward the door to the artifact library. I needed to get through the door. Hopefully, the extra security would hold her off until I could find something back there to fight her off with.

But the wind was suddenly behind me, pushing me toward the witch.

I couldn't stop myself from moving toward her.

I grabbed onto the counter, my feet flying up into the air as the wind increased. If I let go I would fly right at her.

My fingers ached in an effort to keep from being drawn toward Felicity.

They started to slip.

The book, a fear-filled voice said in my ear. *Use the book*.

I had no idea where the voice was coming from. I didn't know why I could hear it in my head. I didn't know who it was. But I was out of options. I reached for the book, straining mightily to touch it.

But I couldn't reach it. And my fingers began to let go.

The door behind Felicity opened and Lea stood there, a murderous look on her face. "Felicity Quilleran, get thee gone from this place!" She threw her hands into the air and blasted the Quilleran witch with a double beam of energy.

The light hit some kind of barrier and sizzled, framing Felicity like a fiery hoop in a circus act. The wind died down to a breeze again and my feet hit the ground.

But it started to build again almost immediately.

And worse, Felicity was heading for Lea, an oily ball of black energy sizzling in each hand.

Use the book! the voice in my head screamed at me.

I decided I had nothing to lose. "Down!" I screamed to Lea, and then I dove for the space beneath the counter.

I didn't look, didn't take the time to move the book. I slapped my palm over the picture of the lightning bolt and hit the ground as the energy roared away. I jumped to my feet as the energy slammed into Felicity with a meaty smack and shoved her out the door on an explosive roar, leaving behind a fiery trail that died out with a snap and a sizzle.

"Lea!" I shrieked, running for her as the door slammed closed behind the witch.

My friend was lying on the floor, unmoving, her arms protectively covering her head.

"Lea?" I went to my knees beside her, reaching to touch her arm. "Are you okay?"

She slowly started to move, rolling over with a groan. "What in the name of the goddess was that?"

I pulled in a deep, relieved breath. "I have no clue. But I'm really glad it was there." I took Lea's hand, helping her to her feet. "Is anything broken?" I asked my friend, looking her over for any obvious wounds.

She grimaced. "You mean, besides your store?"

My gaze followed hers around the shop. "Blasted Quillerans," I muttered angrily. "Why can't they leave me alone?"

Lea brushed dust off her usual flowy skirt. "I have a few theories on that, but they'll wait for another time." She limped toward the counter. "Is Mr. Wicked okay? The frog?"

Her question spurred my memory. "Frog!" I ran over and looked behind the counter, not seeing the singing bullfrog on the floor or the shelf. I was starting to panic when I opened the door to Wicked's hidey-hole and saw his squishy countenance staring out at me.

"Bawump," he growled out, his thick throat bulging.

"Thank the goddess." I leaned back against the wall. "He's okay."

Lea peeked over the counter, her face registering surprise. "Have you been feeding Mr. Slimy steroids?"

"No, I think he's in the artifact library with Wicked. Felicity brought this guy along with her. She tried to trade him for Mr. Slimy."

Lea nodded. "I take it from the condition of your store you refused?"

"Something like that. Although this guy can apparently belch out Night of the Fairies on command."

Lea's face split into a wide grin. "Really?

Frostbite!"

I opened my mouth to correct her and then decided against it. My friend had been a member of the nerd squad her entire life. Not even being a witch could save her from being considered too odd to be a friend. She'd always tried way too hard to fit in. Unfortunately, that included misusing current slang with aplomb.

She came around the counter and I scooted out of the way as she bent down and scooped the singing frog into her hands. She held him at eye-height to look into his protruding gaze. "Sing Night of the Fairies."

He stared at her for a long moment and then his ugly lips opened. "Bawump."

Lea frowned. "He's broken."

I sighed. "Felicity probably lied to me. I doubt he does anything with that mouth other than snatch bugs out of the air."

My friend continued to stare at the amphibian for a long moment. Finally, she turned to me. "Can I take him?"

I blew air through my lips. "Is a frog ugly?"

Her grin returned. "Thanks, Naida. Let me go put him in a safe spot and I'll come back to help clean this up."

"That's so sweet. Thanks, Lea."

The door opened before Lea and her new, non-singing bullfrog reached it. Sebille walked through, her face paling until her freckles practically glowed. "Caterpillar armpits," she muttered, her eyes wide. "What happened in here?"

"Felicity Quilleran happened," Lea said as she moved past my assistant, heading for the door. "I'll be right back."

"Okay." Then I realized a warning was in order. "Hide all your teacups," I called out. "You have no idea where that butt has been."

Sebille walked across the store with a shell-shocked look on her face. She stared around, a frown taking over her features. "Have I told you that I hate the Quillerans?" she asked.

"Not in the last five minutes."

Dropping her ugly canvas bag onto the counter, she finally met my gaze. "What's with the frog? Are you starting an amphibian-ary."

I bent to pick up a book. "Nope. I'm a frogist, remember. I'm bigoted against the entire frog race, singing or no."

Sebille seemed to consider my words. She opened her mouth as if to ask a question, and then snapped it shut with a shake of her head. "Then why?"

I shrugged. "Who knows. For some reason, they thought I'd be open to a swap."

Sebille rolled her eyes. Then she rolled up her sleeves. "I'll start in the back row."

"Thanks, Sebille."

8

GRANDMOTHER, WHAT BIG TEETH YOU HAVE!

*L*ea and Sebille didn't leave the shop until almost ten at night. By that point we were all shuffling around like extras on a bad zombie film. My lank, grubby hair was hanging in my face and my clothes were covered in dust and cobwebs. It didn't take me long, as I started picking up the books Felicity had thrown about with her power, to realize that everything needed a good cleaning.

What started as a book rescue operation, soon became a Spring-cleaning exercise.

My hands were raw from the wet rag I'd used to wipe everything down, my back was sore and my feet were killing me.

I shuffled into my room above the store and Mr. Wicked trotted in behind me, jumping up onto the bed and hitting his pillow immediately. I glanced into Mr.

Slimy's box and found him staring at me, unblinking. "I brought you a present." I was so tired I barely had the energy to unscrew the lid on the jar I'd carried up, setting it on the bottom of the frog's box and watching as the flies Sebille had trapped wandered out and were snapped from the air by Mr. Slimy's disgusting tongue.

"You're welcome," I said, yawning widely. I glanced toward the kitchen and the bathroom, longing for a snack and a shower but having the energy for only one.

I finally decided my empty stomach was more important than a shower and shuffled toward the kitchen.

Wicked bounded over when I filled his bowls with food and water.

I grabbed a banana from the counter and tried to peel it, discovering I was too weak even to manage that. I grabbed a steak knife from the silverware drawer and lopped off the top of the banana, slicing the peel down the side.

I took a bite, almost too weary to stand.

Something shifted in the air behind me. I went very still as a whisper of sound warned me I wasn't alone.

I swallowed as the shadows emerged from the edges and corners of the room and boiled into a humanoid shape.

Wicked lifted his head from his water bowl and

turned toward the bedroom, his tail snapping. "Meow!"

I squeezed the knife tightly in my fist, letting the banana fall to the counter.

The shape inside the shadows shifted sideways and became clear. I realized I'd been holding my breath and let myself draw air as I recognized my intruder.

The man from the clock tower lowered himself onto a chair in my small living area and stretched out his long legs, peaking his fingers and staring defiantly at me.

"What are you doing in my home?" I asked as anger flared and replaced some of the weariness.

His elbows resting on the armrests of the chair, he pressed the two index fingers of his clasped hands against his lips and continued to stare at me.

I started to feel self-conscious. I picked up my banana and pretended to focus on that.

After a moment he decided to respond. "You're in very great danger."

I blew a raspberry, which would have been much more effective if I hadn't blown a chunk of banana out with it.

Wicked pounced on the banana chunk, happily mushing it into the throw rug and then looking at the bit stuck to one claw with obvious alarm.

The goofy cat shot straight into the air and hit

the floor running, apparently trying to outrun the mushy banana on his claw.

I fought a grin at his antics.

Mr. No Name didn't bother fighting his. "He's quite charming."

"Yes." The word came out bathed in venom. "You haven't told me your name. Not that I care. But I need to know what to call you. Unless you've grown fond of Mr. Slimy."

He blinked in surprise. "Rustin. Have I done something to anger you?"

"Have you done something to anger me?" I mocked in his annoyingly snotty tone. "You mean, like bringing the wrath of the Quilleran family down on me, Rustin?"

He frowned. "That wasn't my intent, I assure you."

"Then why don't you tell me what your intent was?"

"Are you not the keeper of the artifacts?"

The first niggles of doubt found me and I turned away to dump the peel into the trash as I avoided responding.

"Naida?"

"Yes." I turned back, crossing my arms over my chest. "I wrangle artifacts by magical vocation."

He nodded. "I have brought you information on an artifact that needs to be corralled. I thought you'd be pleased."

I scrubbed a hand over my face so I wouldn't snap at him. He was right to have brought me the information. I was being a witch. But not in the traditional sense. I only *wished* I had a witch's powers. "Okay, what's the deal with the frog and the book, exactly?"

"The book is my gift to you. It belonged to an artifact keeper in the thirteenth century. It's been in my...family since the turn of the century."

"A gift, huh? I believe it was in the artifact library before you and your frog showed up."

He pressed his long fingers into his lips for another moment, observing me. There was no judgment on his face. No emotion. He simply seemed to be trying to assess me in some way.

Finally, he inclined his head. "If that's what you choose to believe."

My pitiful stores of energy boiled up and shot to the surface of my fingers, sizzling energetically as I fought for control of my anger.

It would feel so good to zap his hair into upright arrows on his head. I was pretty sure he was an ethereal being so he probably couldn't pee himself. But it was worth a try.

Unfortunately, retribution was an inappropriate use of my inadequate powers. Even horribly undercharged magic users faced energy rebound if they misused their powers.

Reluctantly, I let the magic drain away. "Fine. Where can I find this artifact?"

"The tea infuser is hidden somewhere on the Quilleran property."

My mouth fell open. "Somewhere? You do know their property spans hundreds of acres and includes everything from a volcano to a county-sized lake?" I said in deliberate exaggeration.

He frowned. "I do."

"Can you narrow it down for me?"

"I hope to be able to."

I tapped my foot, waiting.

He finally realized I was waiting. "What?"

"Any time now would be awesome."

"I need to come with you to the property. Once there, I believe I can use sense memory to find it."

"Not a chance."

"I'm afraid you don't have any choice if you want to find the artifact."

I shook my head. "I'll find it. I always do. It just might take a little longer since the knowledge came to me through...non-traditional...means."

I flipped my fingers at him. "You can go now. I'm very tired from cleaning up after your relative's magical tantrum."

His blue gaze went wide. He was surprised I knew he was a Quilleran.

"Yeah, I know. What did you do to make them turn you into a frog?" I asked him.

He scanned a quick look toward Mr. Slimy. "You've met them, right?"

I thought about his question and then nodded. "Point taken." Another question occurred to me. "Have they done this to anyone else?"

He stood up, shrugging as if the question didn't interest him. "I think they might have done it one time before me. An opera singer I think. Poor guy. I heard he still tried to sing the song that had turned him famous after his essence was injected into a frog."

"Help me, goddess," I murmured. I needed to tell Lea she was providing room and board to a deposed male opera singer.

At the very least, she needed to know she shouldn't get naked within bulgy black eye range.

I was dragged from a restful sleep the next morning by the feeling of being watched. My poor sleep-deprived brain went from sub-zero to a hundred in the beat of my opening eyes.

I shrieked and shoved backward, bumping into Wicked on the next pillow and sending him spitting to the end of the bed.

"What are you doing?" I asked the good-looking specter perched next to my bed. Unlike the night before, Rustin the displaced, with a frog clinging to his aura, sat on the air, not bothering to pretend he was corporeal. He sat Indian-style, his long legs crossed and his elbows resting on his knees.

"We need to get going," he told me. "The Quillerans just left the property. They'll be gone for several hours. It's the perfect time to search for the artifact."

I took a deep breath to calm my racing heart and shoved the covers back. I hesitated, realizing I was wearing Disney Princess boxers over an old, one-piece bathing suit. My sleepwear of choice ever since I'd been set afloat on the lake at Camp Wantapot-tyme in sixth grade.

Long story.

I gritted my teeth and swung my legs out, daring Rustin with a glare to comment on my attire. I glanced at the clock, groaning. It was only six o'clock in the morning. Beyond the window over the kitchen sink, the sun was a pink and orange promise on the horizon. "Where on earth are they headed this early in the morning?"

He shrugged, not speaking, which I took to either mean he knew and didn't want to tell me, dang him for being a Quilleran, or he didn't know and didn't want me to know he didn't know.

I stopped, closed my eyes, and tried to untangle that last thought from around my brain so it didn't strangle it.

Then I headed, yawning, toward the bathroom. "Don't snoop while I'm getting dressed."

Twenty minutes later, I stood in front of the magic mirror waiting for Queen Sindra to appear. When she did, she looked as if she'd already been up for hours, her beautiful features smooth and unlined. A smile was like sunlight on her tiny face. "Good morning, Naida. What can I help you with today?"

I quickly filled her in on my predicament and she looked suitably intrigued. "How many do you need?"

"All of them. As many as you can spare today. It's a monumental task."

She nodded. "I understand. We'll be happy to help. To tell you the truth, I've been looking for an excuse to infect the Quilleran's garden anyway."

Grinning, I signed off and turned from the mirror.

Rustin hovered a few inches from the ground behind me. I hadn't seen his reflection in the mirror. He was frowning.

"Do you want to find this artifact, or not?"

He shook his head. "I don't want to risk others. Queen Sindra's people will be in danger."

"The Elves and Fairies are well equipped for danger. And the Sprites have a unique ability to sense rogue magic. I need them if we ever hope to cover all that ground, Rustin."

After a beat, he nodded. "It's actually a good plan."

"Don't sound so surprised."

He smiled sadly.

"Let's go. I want to grab something to eat along the way."

"Wait!"

I turned at the door, frowning a question at him. "What?"

"You have to take the frog."

I grimaced. "Are you sure I have to?"

"Yes. I'm..." anger sparked in his blue eyes. "... tied to him. If you don't take him I can't come."

That had to be a humiliating situation. I almost felt sorry for him. Quilleran or no. "Okay. I'll go get him." I started toward the stairs but stopped as I had a sudden thought. "Do you know how to reverse the spell once we get the infuser?"

Even in his ethereal form I could see the spark of doubt in his gaze. "Yes. I believe I do."

Hm. Why didn't *I* believe he knew how?

9

BIBBIDY-BOBBIDY-BOOM!

I popped the last bite of breakfast sandwich into my mouth and rubbed greasy fingers over my jeans. I glanced over at Sebille, still wishing she hadn't come. "Your mother's going to kill me if anything happens to you," I told my assistant.

She shrugged in her characteristic way. "If that happens, you have my word I'll stick you into a frog so you can live beside a pond for the rest of your squishy, bug-eyed life."

"Very funny. I'll come back from the dead and haunt you."

She grinned. "I think I'll name you Slick."

I stepped out of my car, an ancient Volkswagen bug that was a faded green color where the rust didn't mar its perfection. I'd pulled the car into the woods at the side of the road and we planned to travel to the house on foot. The driveway was inaccessible unless one had a way to get through the massive iron gate. And, though I could probably use my displaced Quilleran to do that, I'd then be trapped inside and they'd have a nice eight by ten photo of Sebille and me entering the property from the cameras scanning the entrance.

I'd rather go on stealth mode, thank you very much.

Besides, I always looked fat in pictures. And my nose got bigger. What's up with that? How does a camera make my nose grow?

Shaking my head to remove the disturbing thought, I grabbed my frog-in-a-box and motioned for Sebille to follow me.

She rolled her eyes and, in a burst of pink light, disappeared. A beat later, a dragonfly buzzed past and Sebille's voice, tiny and indistinct, said something that sounded like, "I see your backside."

I'm fairly certain I misheard her.

Turning partially sideways to hide my backside as I followed (just in case), I broke into a run, heading into the dense woods surrounding the Quilleran home.

On the way there, Sebille and I had discussed the best methods of egress into the house. She'd told me that only the driveway and a quarter-mile on either side of the drive had an actual physical barrier. To the naked, untrained eye, the woods was barrier-free.

However, the miles and miles of acreage around the home, including the woods, was protected by an array of magical barriers. These protections ran the gamut from repelling wards, to blast traps, and even a laser warning system that could only be heard inside the house if triggered.

I was counting on Sebille and Rustin to keep me from triggering any traps, and on my own determination to get me through the mind-altering repelling wards.

And speaking of Rustin...

I glanced down at the frog-in-a-box and frowned. "Are you going to join us?"

"Ribbit."

My frown deepened. "Any day now..."

"Ribbit!" Mr. Slimy gave a little sideways hop that caused him to bounce off the grease spot at the side of the box and then settled back onto his moss.

I sighed. "Okay then, the ghost is a no-show. Awesome Possum."

A tiny projectile buzzed past my ear and I lifted a hand to swipe it away. Just in time, I remembered why I shouldn't immediately swipe at any bug-like critters in the air. At the moment, some of my best friends were bugs.

A long tongue snaked out of the donut box and snagged the buzzing intruder.

I grimaced. "Hopefully, you didn't just eat Sebille, Quilleran."

A tinny voice sounded to my right and I turned to find Rustin, sort of, blipping in and out like a bad hologram.

I stopped, trying to read his lips as his voice faded in and out, his hands moving as he spoke.

"Yeah, I'm not getting any of this," I told him. "What's up with the short-circuiting act?"

He stopped trying to talk to me, his shoulders slumping. He flashed away and reappeared right in front of me.

I gave a girly little scream, my cheeks immediately heating with embarrassment. "Don't sneak up on a girl," I scolded.

He frowned back at me, pointing down at the ground beneath his shadowy feet.

I followed the direction he was pointing and saw nothing. But he seemed so insistent that I squinted at the spot, finally seeing what looked like an anthill underneath the leaves and scrub grass.

I crouched down, placing my hand above the hill, palm down, and felt the magical energy throbbing off of it.

"Blast trap," I said, straightening. "Thanks."

Rustin nodded and disappeared again.

I walked on. The woods were quiet except for the occasional buzz of a hapless bug, some of which succumbed to the mighty tongue of my frog-in-a-box when they buzzed too close.

I was starting to think I should dip that thing in gold when Slimy passed and hang it on my wall. That long, sticky tongue was a more effective killing machine than any magic I'd ever seen.

A deep, stomach-clenching feeling of foreboding filled me as I moved closer to the house. My steps slowed. My heart rate picked up. More and more, I found myself snapping fearful glances around the area as I walked, my mind creating monsters based on nothing other than my fertile imagination.

After a while, I realized I must be feeling the effects of the repelling ward. I pushed past it, despite the greasy fear-sweat coating my face and the reluctance dogging my steps. Finally, I stepped through a tree line and the world opened up in front of me.

Literally.

The green, rolling grounds were the antithesis of the forest I'd just traversed. Open, breezy, and beautiful beyond reality.

I recognized magic-enhanced beauty when I saw it.

The repelling ward snapped away with a soft ping and my lungs expanded on the first, good breath I'd taken since entering the woods.

I felt good. Too good. Remembering the task ahead, I tried to shove my optimism back a few notches. All was not as good as it currently felt.

I was probably just suffering magical buoyancy from my repelling ward reprieve.

I glanced around, looking for Rustin.

No Rustin. His family must have warded against his forays outside the frog. I sighed. I'd brought the stupid frog for nothing.

I started jogging toward the house, feeling silly carrying my donut box with me. But I couldn't leave it behind. I had no idea which way I'd be going when I left.

There was no way I was giving the Quillerans their frog back. Accidentally or on purpose.

I was halfway to the house when my foot landed on something that crunched loudly and I jerked to a stop as a sulfurous fog lifted from the ground.

I had an instant to consider what had just happened before I felt the energy rising along my legs and suddenly knew. "Caterpillar whiskers!" I screamed, flinging the donut box as far away as I could, just as the explosion hit.

Scalding energy boiled up from the earth, scraping across my legs and burning me through the heavy denim of my jeans. I felt the canvas in my sneakers giving out and my toes flaming up like roman candles through the breach.

The energy gathered beneath me until the pressure was too great and then it propelled me into the air, sending me airborne for a dozen yards before disappearing with a squeaky whimper of dying power. I hung in the air for half a breath, and then dropped like a bad souffle, smacking into the ground.

I lay there groaning as an insistent ringing sound filled my ears. The sound pinged through my auditory channels, pressing into my brain like probing fingertips.

I felt the vibration of my groans in my chest and throat, but I couldn't hear them.

All I could hear was that damnable ringing.

My face was smashed into the grass. My bones felt like dust as I lay there, agony filtering up from my firecracker toes and sweeping over my legs.

A deep, rhythmic booming sound slowly entered my auditory sphere and I realized it was the sound of my heart beating.

Well, that was a positive at least.

I moved and agony razored through me.

Maybe it was a positive. The jury was still out.

The booming receded and other sounds slowly took its place.

Birds sang happily in the sky above my head. Bugs buzzed. Frogs croaked. Bugs buzzed.

Bugs...buzzed...

I swatted in irritation at the frantic whirring above my ear.

"Naida! Get off the ground and let's get this done."

Ah yes. Miss Compassion had arrived.

I groaned again and could almost feel her impatience. "Man up, keeper. You have an artifact to wrangle."

I rolled over and looked up at the tiny, insect-sized version of my non-compassionate assistant. "You do know I could squash you like a bug right now?"

Sebille buzzed sideways and then back so quickly my brain turned to liquid from the movement. I was pretty sure if she didn't stay still I was going to have a seizure. "Stop moving."

"You mean like this?" She shot skyward and then back down, so quickly she was just a tiny, irritating blur on the air.

"I hate you so much right now."

Sebille chuckled. "Seriously though. Walk it off, Naida. We need to get into that house and find the artifact."

She was right. The search had to go on, despite the fact that I was a cat's whisker away from death at the moment. I gritted my teeth and pushed to my feet, staring down at my newly exposed toes.

Sebille buzzed closer and looked down at them too. "Why am I getting a hankerin' for grilled hot dogs right now?"

"You suck," I mumbled, hobbling forward on my fried-sausage toes. "What's the report from the grounds? Has your mother found anything there?"

"She found a litter of kittens that look a lot like Mr. Wicked."

I stopped and stared into her tiny, disgusted face. "We need to save them."

"Already underway. They were locked in a small building near the pond. The Fairies released them and Mother ordered them taken to a safe spot."

I closed my eyes, simultaneously relieved and terrified. When I thought about how much the Quillerans had tortured me over Mr. Wicked, I knew they'd be handing out great dollops of misery over the loss of the rest of the litter. "Good." I hobbled forward again.

Sebille whirred forward and then back, hanging on the air in front of my face looking disgusted.

"What?" I snarled.

"Can't you move any faster? At this rate I'll spend the rest of my life on this task. I'd hoped to get married and have children someday."

I shuddered at the thought of mini-Sebilles scurrying around haranguing me. "I'm going as fast as I can. In case you hadn't noticed, my feet are only a squirt of mustard and a spoon full pickle relish away from being totally bar-b-cued."

She sighed, the tiny wisp of air blowing her bright red bangs off her face. "Hold on."

I stopped and followed her movement toward my toes with alarm. "What are you doing?"

I took two clumsy steps back, certain she was

going to lop off my toes or something equally unfeeling and desperate to remove the problem.

"Just stand still," her small voice filtered up to me. "I got this."

A soft, pink light emerged from her tiny form as she hovered above my toes. It bathed the burned digits in gentle illumination, soothing and easing some of the swelling. Her wings pulsed three times and dust filtered down onto my charbroiled flesh. It healed slightly, though the skin was still an angry red.

She shot back upward and looked into my face. "There. Try that."

I nodded, took a step forward, and fell right on my face.

10

A PRICKLY SITUATION

"You have a little grass, just there..." Sebille told me on a grin.

I glared at her, digging at my teeth with a fingernail to extract the piece of lawn. "You could have told me my toes would be numb."

She shrugged, landing on a dust-covered table in the giant entryway. I'd had a sneezing fit when we'd opened the massive front door of the castle-like home. A light breeze drifted through the door when we opened it, sending dust sifting into the air from every surface.

I set frog-in-a-box on the table a couple of feet away from Sebille, just in case Super Tongue the Green Avenger decided she looked tasty. "I could maybe find it in myself to someday forgive the Quillerans for being giant douche-nozzles." I said.

"But they should be buried up to their ears in a fire ant colony for their housekeeping."

Sebille had been pinching her nose shut since we'd come through the door. "So true."

The stench inside the home bespoke the witchy family's dubious activities, a decidedly sulfurous odor hung on the air and the dust littering nearly every surface glittered with unspent power.

"Where do we start?" Sebille asked.

I closed my eyes and extended my arms, pulling my artifact-sensing energy forward and sending it out into the home. I opened my eyes to see the glossy tendrils of seeking energy dispersing along the first floor and oozing up the steps to the second.

We waited for one of the tendrils to chime in discovery. After a moment, a gentle, tinkling sound filled the air. I pointed up the stairs. "That way."

Another chime sounded. We glanced toward the dark hallway leading away from us. "You look up. I'll look down," I told Sebille.

Another chime tinkled, and another, and another. Soon the entire house chimed a cacophony of discovery.

Sebille and I shared a look. I'd had magical misfires before. And I'd had multiple discoveries before. But never anything of the current magnitude for either.

"They must have an entire library of stolen artifacts," I told Sebille. I was beginning to think the

Book of Blank Pages that Rustin's family had "found" might have been gained in a less harmless fashion than he'd implied.

She frowned, glancing toward a distant chime that sounded anew, seeming to set off a whole new round of fresh alerts.

I sighed. "I guess we're going to have to do this the old-fashioned way."

Sebille nodded. "I'll start upstairs." She buzzed away so fast I almost couldn't track her as she zipped up the stairs.

Sighing, I headed for the kitchen, figuring that would be the best place to start.

An hour later, Sebille and I stood staring down at a pile of tea infusers on the kitchen table, our expressions dire.

Full size again, Sebille shook her head. "Who has this many tea infusers?"

"Apparently the Quillerans aren't good at sharing." No surprise there. Nobody knew exactly how many of the evil rabbits lived in the big house. Some estimates had them at twenty assorted siblings, cousins, aunts and uncles. Sebille and I had rummaged through ten obviously inhabited bedrooms in our search.

There were another half dozen that could have been inhabited, but they looked like temporary stopping places at best. Like fancy, albeit dusty, hotel rooms for visiting evil spawn.

"I guess we need to take them all?" Sebille looked doubtful.

I shared her concern. My artifact-sensing magics had pinged on every single one of the infusers. Either my energies had become skewed in the big house, most likely due to warding if that was the case, or the Quillerans had found a way to duplicate the artifact.

Though I didn't have high hopes for the batch. None of them seemed to have an excess of magical energy attached to them.

"I don't think we have any choice," I agreed. "Maybe once we get them out of here we can figure out which infuser is the culprit."

"You'd think there'd be some residue of essence left behind in them," Sebille said on a frown.

"Yeah. You'd think." I tugged a plastic bag from my pocket, snapping it open. "Let's do this and get out of here. This place gives me the creeps."

We started shoving infusers into the bag. Across the room, a soft sound drew my attention. I turned my head just as a large kitchen knife flew through the air, aimed right at Sebille.

I shrieked, flinging myself at my assistant and sending us both to the floor. The blade sliced through the thickness of my denim jacket, leaving the telltale burn of a wound behind.

I gasped at the pain, giving my arm a quick look

as a veritable army of knives and sharp tined forks flew in our direction.

All across the room, drawers flew open and deadly utensils flew out, aiming unerringly at us.

We scurried under the table, hearing the lethal projectiles thump against the wood of the top and legs as we crawled quickly away.

"Get small!" I screamed at Sebille. She nodded and flashed into bug size in the blink of an eye. She shot out from under the table and a bright light suddenly flared through the room.

Every projectile in the room stopped in mid-air and, with a whisper of dying magic, clanked to the floor. I didn't waste any time. Crawling quickly from under the table, I took off running.

A muffled thump in the direction of the stairs had me screeching to a halt. Sebille froze next to me, her wings a colorful blur on the air. "What is that?" I asked the Sprite.

She frowned, her eyes narrowing on the odd-looking conglomeration of metal and cloth.

Whatever it was, it had a sword clutched in one, metal hand and it was coming right for us.

Across the entry, a door slammed open and a long, metal object with a pointy end flew through, stopping a few feet from the door and hovering there.

The fireplace poker was aimed right at my heart.

A sword flew from the same room a beat later, taking up a spot in front of the exit. An assortment of athame flew from the upstairs rooms and surrounded us, curved blades forming a perfect circle on the air.

And last, but definitely not least, a door in the hallway slammed open and dozens of round, flat, objects that gave off a sulfurous stench and were about two inches in diameter each, flew into the room and dropped to the ground, forming an impenetrable path toward the exterior door.

"What are those?" I asked Sebille.

"Blast traps," she breathed, tension showing in the jerky rhythm of her wings.

"Slug snot," I responded. "We're trapped."

Naida?

The voice was faint, broken, but I recognized it as Rustin trying to break through. I glanced around, looking for his shadowy form in the entryway.

I found him, finally. Like his voice, his form was so faint I could barely make out his features. "Help us!" I said softly, afraid if I spoke too loudly the current hiatus from death would end.

He moved suddenly, blipping closer and I could see his lips moving but I couldn't hear what he said.

"I can't hear you," I said, my tone betraying my nerves as I kept an eye on the death-squad of household furnishings and deadly blades surrounding us.

Two lines of frustration appeared between his barely opaque gaze. He lifted his hand and closed it into a fist, flinging his fingers open with a muttered command I read on his lips.

The air before me shimmered and the blank-paged book appeared. I barely caught it before it fell.

My movement caused a ripple in the force and the strange deathtrap jerked into motion.

Sebille sent a blast of white energy into the air but it didn't stop the deadly conglomeration of stuff.

I closed my eyes, expecting death, but a heartbeat later the utensils jerked to a halt, mere inches away. They throbbed on the air as if a whisper away from surging into motion again.

Rustin's lips were moving and the pages of the book were flying. I couldn't read his words on his lips, but I recognized his hand gestures.

He wanted me to use the book.

But how?

The last page in the book flicked into place and the pages started back the other way, moving more quickly as if tied to the frantic flow of blood through my veins.

Rustin's face clearly showed his concern. He glanced around the room as if he saw clearly the predicament we were in. But I had no idea what to do.

I watched the pages flip, praying they would land on a solution as they'd done before. But they reached the front of the book and started back through again.

"What do I do?" I asked him, desperation filling my tone.

He hung his head, his muscles straining.

I turned to Sebille. "Go. Get your mother," I whispered.

Sebille shook her head. "If I move they'll attack."

The pages continued to flicker so quickly I was starting to worry the book would tear itself apart.

The army of threatening blades quivered on the air and shot closer a couple more inches.

We were running out of time.

Looking at the strained expression on Rustin's face, I realized he was probably holding it all back, but he couldn't do it forever. I figured he was already fighting just to appear in the warded home, and if he was also controlling the book...

Then I realized. He couldn't be controlling the book. If he was, we'd have already come to a solution.

That meant that I...

Making a sudden decision, I did the only thing I could think of to do. "Book, I need an exit."

The pages quivered, the flickering slowed, and they finally stopped, near the front of the tome.

A picture of a door appeared.

The knives quivered again. With a sudden whoosh of sulfur-threaded air, the tension left the atmosphere and I realized Rustin had lost his hold on the blades.

"Touch the page!" I screamed to Sebille. I couldn't wait to see if she listened, I slammed my palm onto the page and flashed into nothingness just as the first blades smacked into the magical book, turning it to a pincushion before it even hit the floor.

11

SANCTUARY FOR KITTIES

I landed in the grass next to my car. I was breathing fast and hard, my heart pounding dangerously against my ribs. I leaned against the car, fighting to get my breathing under control.

A loud, whirring sound had me whipping around to find a veritable army of Fae approaching me at a rapid clip. I would have panicked, but I saw Queen Sindra leading the way.

She whirred to a stop in front of me. "What happened?" she demanded, hands on hips. Her face was contorted with anger, her tone imperious.

I pulled another breath into my lungs. "We were attacked. It must have been some kind of magical warding. We barely escaped."

Sindra's anger eased a bit. "How did you escape?"

"The book," I gasped out, wishing my heart would stop beating so fast. "Rustin sent me the book and it gave us a door."

She cocked her head. "Book? What book?" Oops. I'd committed magical blabbery. Big mistake. Rule number one in the magical world, never reveal any more about your tools than absolutely necessary. Theft of mystical tools ran rampant and it was never a good idea to let your enemies know too much about how you worked. They tended to use it against you.

Even your friends might become a liability if they knew too much.

I shrugged, cultivating careful blank face. "I don't know. It's something he has. A witch trick."

Sindra grimaced as I knew she would. Anything tied to the witchy world was abhorrent to the Fae. "Well, whatever it was, it was powerful. We were expelled too."

Ah. That explained the indignant rage. Queens didn't like being forced to do things against their will. "Sorry. It couldn't be helped." I hesitated only a beat and then forced myself to ask... "Did you find any artifacts?"

She crossed her tiny arms over her chest. "No. Only the cats." She frowned. "They're a pitiful group."

My heart broke. "Where did you take them?"

Her gaze slid past my shoulder, toward the car. I felt my stomach twist. Turning slowly, I saw a pair of dark-gold eyes staring out at me through the back window. As I looked, another pair of eyes, and then another, and another appeared.

My heart sank. I couldn't take them all. It would be much too dangerous. I'd have wall-to-wall Quillerans beating down my doors to get to them. But looking at their sad, pitiful little faces I knew I wouldn't be able to turn them away. I'd find a solution.

Somehow.

The force of Fae rippled behind Sindra and a Sprite dressed in the signature uniform of one of the Queen's guards flew forward, stopping mid-air in front of her and bowing low. "My Queen. We have a crisis."

I nearly rolled my eyes. So, what else was new?

Yeah, I'd been hanging out with Sebille too long.

Sebille!

I looked frantically around as Sindra conferred with her guard in a language I didn't understand. Why hadn't Sebille come out with me? Had she ignored my command to hit the book?

Panic washed through me. She had to be okay. She had to be...

The queen turned back to me. "We must go. The Enchanted Forest has been breached."

I nodded, my mind preoccupied with Sebille's absence. "Thank you for your help."

The Queen inclined her head and motioned for her army to move out.

Torn between the need to get the kittens to a safe place and the need to find Sebille, I barely noticed their departure.

In the end, I decided Sebille was better equipped to take care of herself than the kittens. And, with a sour feeling in my stomach that I was making a terrible mistake, I climbed into the bug and got out of there.

There was only one place where I figured the kittens would be safe. It should have been my last choice, given the owner's attachment to the witching world. But LeeAnn Mapes, called LA by her friends, was a friend of mine and I trusted her completely.

Her new boyfriend, the witch, was another story. He was still an unknown quantity to me. And he was a witch.

'Nuff said?

Illusion City was about a thirty-minute drive from my small town of Enchanted. I made the drive covered in cats. It wasn't a bad way to travel. The cats were breaking my heart. They were too skinny, their fur unkempt and their manner toward me wary.

It was clear they hadn't been well taken care of and it made me hate the Quillerans even more. There were four of them. They were all a shade of gray similar to Mr. Wicked's and had light-gold to nearly orange eyes. Each cat wore a slender leather collar around its small neck, a magical symbol hanging from each one. I was hoping LA could tell me what the symbols meant. I had a feeling they were dark arts talismans, but I was praying I was wrong.

I flew past the sign announcing the outskirts of Illusion City and slowed, eyeing the cross streets as I drove to find the one leading to LA's home and sanctuary. She lived in an older neighborhood on the edge of the city, in an old Victorian that had probably once been a stunning home for a well-to-do family. The homes were still beautiful, though a little worn around the edges. Many of them had undergone rehabilitation, making the neighborhood a popular spot for growing families.

I turned left onto LA's street and drove past an array of houses similar to hers. They were set fairly close together, on small lots that were mostly taken up by oversized trees. I spotted her home about two-thirds of the way along the street and stopped the VW bug at the curb. The home was a freshly painted brown and cream with light blue trim. The front door was a creamy beige to match the house and I could see the haze of protective warding overshadowing it.

I wondered if LA would accept the four cats into her sanctuary. I realized it was asking a lot. I'd made a deliberate decision not to call ahead and ask if she'd take the orphaned felines, thinking it would be better to present their adorable pitifulness to her in the flesh.

It would be harder to say no at that point.

Yeah, I know that was a little sneaky. But, hey, desperate times...

After some thought, I grabbed the smallest kitten and headed for the front door. I knocked loudly, scanning the street as I wondered which house belonged to Deg, LA's boyfriend, the witch.

Heavy footsteps sounded on the other side of the door. I hugged the kitten closer and turned expectantly, finding stunningly good-looking man with mahogany hair and dark silver eyes staring out at me. "Can I help you?"

"Oh. Um..."

"Who is it, Deg?"

My friend came up behind her gorgeous witch and grinned. "Naida!" She pushed past the unhappy-looking man and enveloped me in a hug. "How are you? And who's this little cutie?"

LA fixed her changeable blue-green gaze on the kitten and her eyes lit up. "May I?"

I nodded, handing her over.

"Oh!" LA turned to Deg. "Look. Isn't she adorable?"

Deg eyed the kitten with a frown on his handsome face and I couldn't help wondering why.

"She's one of several kittens we rescued. I was wondering if you would mind adding them to the sanctuary for a while? Just until I figure out what to do with them?"

LA and Deg shared a look and I tensed. LA didn't look pleased at the idea.

"Is it a problem?" I asked. "Because if it is..."

LA shook her head, her long, bright red hair swinging around her small face. "No, it's not that." Her gaze slid to Deg's again. "How many are in this litter?"

I chewed the inside of my lip, ready to turn around and leave.

LA must have seen the flight response in my gaze. She reached out and clasped one of my hands. "Let me make this easier. Are these the Quilleran kittens?"

I frowned. "How did you know?"

Deg's frown deepened. He shoved his hands into his pockets. Clearly, he wasn't happy.

LA gave him a warning look. "The web has been retrofitted to include them. They're much too dangerous to leave unattended."

The "web" LA was speaking about was a magical

connection all of the magic users in Illusion City used to keep track of each other. It was far more complex than that, of course, but that was as much as I knew about it.

"Yes. They were being mistreated and used for dark magic. I had to rescue them, LA." Had that whining tone really come from me?

She nodded, handing the kitten to Deg, who, despite his unhappy demeanor, immediately softened as the sleepy kitten snuggled against his chest. "Let's go get the others. They're not safe on the street."

***

I sat on the floor of LA's fragrant, warm kitchen, watching the kittens play as she brewed up a concoction of special milk that she said would be good for their coats and for getting rid of any parasites they might have collected.

"They were being kept in a building on the grounds. Queen Sindra and her people rescued them."

LA nodded. "Don't you have a kitten from this litter?"

"Mr. Wicked." I smiled. "He's really smart." By smart, I meant he was well-attuned to magic. He and his litter-mates had been bred to be conduits for witch magic. Being a cat-shifting familiar, LA knew what I meant.

She shook her head. "Such a shame. Some witches don't understand the value of a good magic conduit, let alone how to treat them humanely." She flicked Deg a look and he nodded.

"These cats are valuable beyond compare. Which is why the Quillerans won't stop until they get them back." He balled up a piece of paper and flicked it to the floor for the kittens to chase. "And why we need to keep the kittens away from them at all costs."

Hope filled my breast. "I agree." I watched silently as LA placed a large bowl of the special milk on the floor. The kittens ran over and stuck their heads into the bowl, lapping happily at it.

LA smiled down at them. After a moment, she looked up. "I take it you're looking for an artifact?"

I nodded. "A tea infuser that apparently removes a person's essence when it's used. I have a frog at home right now that tells me he was once a Quilleran."

Both Deg and LA looked shocked.

"They went after one of their own?" Deg asked. "I can't believe it."

"That's a bad bunch," LA said. She looked down at the kittens again, her expression softening.

I realized how much danger I was putting LA and her friends in. "Look, I know I'm asking a lot..."

LA shook her head. "This is what the sanctuary is for. I'll keep them. But I do need your permission to find them good homes."

My pulse spiked. I hadn't realized until that moment that I'd been considering keeping them all. Wicked would love having his brothers and sisters around. "Oh. Well, okay. But maybe keep one of them. I might want to take a sibling home for Wicked."

"Done," LA said, grinning.

"And you need to tell us why the collars all have sigils on them," Deg added in a suspicious tone.

I shook my head. "I wish I knew."

We all looked at the four collars lying on the surface of the table. Each one had a small artifact hanging from the loop like a bauble. There was an athame replica on one, a pentacle on another, what looked like a focus sigil on the third, and the symbol for chaos magic on the fourth. I suddenly wondered what symbol Mr. Wicked would have had if they'd managed to hold onto him.

"I'm going to research them," Deg declared as if defying me to argue.

LA gave me an apologetic look after shooting her witch a warning glance. "These sigils tell us what the kittens were being used for. We need the information to protect them and ourselves," she said.

"I'm okay with that," I agreed, catching LA's eye. "I don't want to put you in unnecessary danger. But I thought this might be the last place the Quillerans would look for them."

LA nodded. "We'll mask their location as best we can. But the sooner you find your artifact the better. If you take away their ability to use the cats, they'll hopefully lose interest in them."

12

BLEEP YE MATEY, YE'RE THE DEVIL'S BLEEP

*B*y the time I walked back into my shop I was already dead on my feet and the day was only half over. To say I wasn't prepared for the next surprise in my life was an understatement of gargantuan proportions. Mr. Wicked met me at the front door, though I'd left the connecting door between the artifact library and the shop closed and locked. Unless my kitten had figured out how to unlock doors and open them without opposable thumbs, somebody had breached my warding again.

Frog's cankles! I was getting sick of people invading my space.

I scooped up Mr. Wicked and glanced around the shop, seeing nothing out of place.

Moving quietly to the dividing door, I listened for telltale noises, hearing nothing. Mr. Wicked wriggled to be released so I settled him on the floor.

He bounded ahead of me into the artifact library, hopping up onto Shakespeare's desk and dancing away from the dripping ink quill that flew off its surface, heading for the chair which was, unfortunately not filled with the writer the pen expected.

It shot across the room and slammed into the wooden frame of the communicating mirror, dropping to the floor.

Wicked jumped onto the shelves which held thousands of artifacts, large and small, and pawed at the metal support leg, his orange gaze locked on the handle of the deadly sword sticking out from the top shelf.

I looked up to Edward Teach's sword and grimaced. Better known as Blackbeard, Teach and his pirate crew had tormented merchants around the West Indies and North America in the late sixteen hundreds. His sword was on the topmost shelf where all the most dangerous artifacts lived, well out of reach of someone's inadvertent grasp. Sebille and I had named the bright-eyed parrot sitting on the blade Sewer Beak, SB for short, because his speech was heavily weighted with words a bloodthirsty pirate would have found useful upon a pirate's ship.

The fact that Mr. Wicked was basically recommending that I grab the sword didn't speak well of what was waiting for me upstairs.

I resisted the idea, looking around for something less...deadly to protect myself with. But Wicked yowled softly, his orange gaze shooting toward the ceiling high above our heads.

Sighing, I reached out a hand and engaged my artifact seeking magic, which worked as a locator when I couldn't actually see the artifact, and as a magnet when I could.

The sword lifted off the shelf, sending SB into the air in a fit of squawking and foul language, and drifted to my hand, well-worn wooden handle first.

My fingers wrapped around the hilt like it belonged to me, the handle magically adjusting to the size of my palm and length of my digits.

With a final flurry of magically expunged sewer language, SB landed on my shoulder, hopping unhappily back and forth from foot to foot as he worried at my hair with his curved beak.

"Leave it, SB!" I told the cranky parrot. He gave me a theatrical sigh. "Bossy ye be for a wee female, lass."

"Arrr! I not be wee and I not be bossy, ye scurvy blackguard," I countered, heading for the steps. "I be wanting to keep my hair attached to my head." I bit my lip against further speech, realizing the sword had already pervaded me to the point that I was talking pirate gibberish.

An unfortunate side effect, which I defeated with a flick of shielding magic.

Wicked took off across the room, no doubt to hide until our intruders were gone. I started up the stairs, the sword clutched in two hands, and SB singing a lewd tavern song as I tried to shush him.

In response, the parrot threw back his bright green head and caterwauled, off-key and loud enough to make my ears ring. "Ye bloody Brit sons of blessed mums whose gifts to ye be small, ye'll fall to Blackbeard's mighty sword, 'fore yer mum's tears of shame can fall."

"SB!" I whispered harshly. "Be. Quiet!"

The parrot shifted from foot to foot on my shoulder, turning in a circle as I carefully sidestepped a creaking stair. "What ye be afraid of, lass? Ye've the mighty Blackbeard's sword. The blood of yonder scurvy dogs is all but spilt."

So much for sneaking up on whatever, or whoever waited for me in my rooms.

A floorboard above my head creaked and I went very still, listening.

"Ye busty barmaids, ale in hand..."

"Oh for...!" I swept my hand over my shoulder in an attempt to expel the loudly singing parrot. Unfortunately for me, he flapped his wings and took to the air, only to land again on my other shoulder before I reached the door.

I took a deep breath, realizing the jig was up, and stepped into the open doorway, sword held in front of me in both hands.

My knuckles were white.

My heart was pounding.

My parrot was swearing.

I sucked in a quiet gasp.

Four Quilleran witches stood arrayed in a half-circle in front of my couch. Though their eyes were wide as SB opened his beak and belched out a few more lyrics to his bawdy song, each new line raunchier than the last, I felt their power like a thick, sulfurous fog filling my lungs.

There was so much magic in the room it was hard to draw a full breath. Sweat broke out on my temples and coated my palms. I squeezed the handle of the sword harder to keep it from slipping out of my grasp. "Get out of my house."

My voice came out with a harsh, booming quality that I knew was another side effect of the sword. In that moment, as I saw the four witches stiffen with alarm, I was glad of that particular side effect.

The dying sunlight outside my kitchen window fell across the room between us like a barrier, its gilded rays catching the razor-sharp edge of Blackbeard's sword and making it spark as if from magical energy.

The Quillerans shifted backward without moving their feet.

I glanced at Felicity, happy to see a sheen of sweat on her brow too. Maybe she was as scared of me as I was of them. "Did you not learn your lesson the last time?"

Felicity twitched, her unattractive face folding into a frown. "We want our litter back."

I tried for an expression of confusion, but I was pretty sure I didn't entirely pull it off. "Litter? I don't know..."

"Don't lie to us," Jacob Quilleran boomed.

His voice ricocheted around my small apartment, rippling over my skin like cool water over smooth rocks. Despite my best intentions to seem intimidating, I jumped slightly at the sound.

The patriarch of the Quilleran clan was an imposing figure. He stood in the center of the group, a good foot taller and half again as wide as the three women. He wasn't fat. Not by a long stretch. He was about six feet four and two hundred fifty pounds of pure muscle. And if his magical abilities had physical attributes, they'd be similarly endowed. "You have twenty-four hours to return them to us."

"Or what?" I asked, clearing my throat as it caught on the words.

Candace Quilleran anchored one end of the half-circle. Her thin, cruel mouth twisted upward at the corners, scaring me until I realized it was supposed to be a smile. She held Mr. Slimy's donut box up for me to see. "Missing something, sorceress?"

My heart stuttered. The sword lowered a few inches as I tried to process my surprise. *Frog's cankles*! It was Rustin, or to be more precise, Mr. Slimy. I'd left him behind when I'd made my unplanned exit from the Quilleran home. With everything that was going on, I'd totally forgotten him.

I'm so sorry, Rustin.

I forced myself to swallow and pasted an unconcerned look on my face. "My breakfast bagels?" I shook my head. "I ate them. They were yummy."

Candace's smile drooped, her yellow eyes flashing. "It seems you left something in the box. I was thinking of cooking it up for my dinner. I've heard frog's legs are delicious."

The woman standing next to her nodded. I thought her name was Margot. She was a Quilleran cousin, and she was known throughout Enchanted and the surrounding area as the enforcer. She stood several inches taller than the other two women. She was strongly made, standing on muscular legs encased in stretchy yoga pants and wearing a sleeveless tee that emphasized her muscular arms. She wore her coal-black hair skimmed straight back from her face, ruthlessly cinched in a ponytail at the back of her thick neck.

Her eyes were the expected Quilleran yellow, but there were visible flecks of green that flashed with energy. I realized most of the clogging magic energy in the room came from her and Jacob. The other two were relatively powerless compared to them. "You'll have to excuse her ignorance, dear cousin," she said, her gaze never leaving mine. "I believe Naida has lost something and hasn't yet grasped the significance of her loss." She held my gaze and extended her hand, dropping a long coil of silky red onto the floor. "And if she doesn't do as we command, she's about to lose a whole lot more."

As my horrified gaze slid downward, to the bright red coil of hair lying between us on the carpet, the Quillerans disappeared from my apartment like a quartet of ugly spirits.

I barely notice their departure.

I dropped to my knees, the sword thumping forgotten to the carpet beside me. Reaching for the bright red strand of hair, I swallowed hard, my pulse pounding in my ears.

They'd taken Sebille.

I barely had time to register the fact that the Quillerans had my assist...no, my friend. I had to admit that to myself. Sebille was my friend. Though a very annoying one.

No sooner had I settled that fact in my mind than I heard the jangle of the bell downstairs. I swore softly, realizing I'd left the book shop unlocked.

"Naida? Are you up there?"

I closed my eyes with relief when I heard Lea's voice. "Yes. Hold on. I'm coming down."

I stood and headed toward the door, SB disappearing through the door ahead of me in a shower of brightly colored feathers.

I grimaced as bright red and blue feathers hit my carpet and wondered if the undead parrot was molting due to too many years in magical limbo.

I clutched Sebille's silky hair in my fist and brushed at tears as I bounded down the stairs, entering the bookstore to find Lea standing stock-still in the center of the room, twisting her fingers together.

"What's wrong?" I asked my friend, my own bad news dying on my lips at the obvious evidence of hers.

Lea stopped pacing and reached for my hands, squeezing them hard. "Where's Sebille?"

I felt my face folding into sadness. "She's..." I took a deep breath and forced the word past my lips. "I think the Quillerans have her."

Tears filled Lea's eyes. She pulled me into an unexpected hug. "Oh, Naida. I'm so sorry."

I held up the silky strand of hair and gave Lea the brief rundown of our failed exploration of the Quilleran home and my adventure upstairs.

A vibrant rainbow flapped past overhead, feathers raining down to get stuck in my and Lea's hair. SB landed on the uppermost shelf and twitched his wings, dancing from foot to foot. "Blast ye blackguards straight to *bleep*...Ye're the devil's *bleep* and I'll see ye boiling in a pot of yer own *bleepety bleep* blood!"

Lea's eyebrows lifted at the Parrot's unconventional contribution to the conversation. "Is that parrot being magically bleeped?"

I nodded, feeling bereft and sad. "I think the previous KoA developed the spell because she got tired of hearing him curse like a sailor."

Lea nodded. "Remind me to look into that. I have an acquaintance who deserves to be bleeped."

I nodded. "You came here to tell me something?"

She rubbed a hand over her forehead, shoving tawny hair aside. "I intercepted a message in my scrying globe a little while ago. Someone's trying to get hold of Sebille. I came over to tell her to check the mirror."

My stomach twisted. "Do you know what it's about?"

Lea sighed, holding an arm across her belly as if she were about to be sick. "I'm afraid so. It looks like Sebille and Rustin aren't the only ones who are suffering the Quillerans' rage. Apparently, they paid a visit to the Enchanted Forest." Lea swallowed hard, fresh tears filling her eyes. "Naida, the Quillerans razed Toadstool City with devastation magic. It's gone. Burned to the ground. All of it. Even Queen Sindra's palace."

13

WHAT BLEEP HATH WE WROUGHT?

I stood in front of the mirror, tears sliding soundlessly down my face. A black and brown, scorched picture of devastation spread from the mirror as far as the eye could see. Fairies darted into the wreckage, pulling out whatever they could find that had survived the attack.

It couldn't have been much.

I prayed there'd been no children in the city when the Quillerans attacked— no ill or aged. And I swore to myself that I would avenge the destruction.

I'd asked to speak to Sindra, but I really hadn't expected her to give me an audience. She had her hands full trying to recover from what had to be an overwhelming experience.

I was shocked when she whirred into view, several guards surrounding her in the face of the new danger.

She looked worn, her pretty face pale where it wasn't smudged with soot and dirt. It didn't surprise me at all that the queen was diving into the work with her subjects. Sprites were a singular breed of magic user, with a different value system than most.

She looked at me, her wings wilted and worn as weariness overcame her tiny frame. Her slim shoulders were slightly bowed under the weight of their loss, but the eyes that found mine carried more than their share of rage. "I understand the witches took my daughter."

I didn't try to soften my response. I realized Sindra would have little patience for it. "Yes. I wanted you to know I'm putting all my resources into finding her. I won't let the Quillerans harm Sebille."

Sindra inclined her head, unsurprised by my declaration. She acted as if it was an expected response on my part. I guessed it was, given that Sebille was both my friend and employee. And I was a trusted member of Queen Sindra's inner circle.

"Lea and I want to help you regroup from the attack. What can we do?"

Sindra ran a pale, smudged hand over her brow. "Nothing. We must take what we can gather and find a new home in the forest."

She must have seen the doubt in my face because she frowned. "What? Speak, Naida."

"It's just that I don't think it's safe there anymore. I think you need to consider relocating to another area entirely."

She didn't look surprised. No doubt she'd had the same thought. "I agree. I've begun negotiations with the council in Illusion City. The Illusory Forest would be a good option for us. But we can't do that today. The sun will be down soon. We must find shelter and protection for the near future."

I chewed my lip. "I might have a solution."

Sindra's dire expression cleared and a flicker of hope lit her gaze. "What is it, Naida? I'm willing to listen to all suggestions."

"It isn't perfect..."

"Nothing will be perfect," she told me. "Right now, I'll settle for good."

I glanced at Lea, who stood out of sight of the mirror, listening. Since she was a witch, she'd thought it would be better for me to present the option to the queen.

I turned back to Sindra. "Lea has a large greenhouse where she grows her herbs and flowers. It's enclosed, heavily warded and will keep your people warm and safe in an environment they'll enjoy. It's not perfect, we'd need to add a fountain for water and we can plant toadstools around the plants, which will take time to grow, but Lea can cast an invisibility spell on the greenhouse, which will be geared specifically against witches. I think it could be a good, short or long-term solution."

Sindra seemed to consider it carefully. After a moment she nodded, some of the tension draining from her face. "Yes. That is more than acceptable. Please tell your friend I am deeply grateful. We'll make sure her plants thrive as long as we live there."

Lea smiled widely, nodding her pleasure that Sindra had accepted.

Sindra's shoulders straightened. "We'll look for the sigil calling us home," she said. "Now I must go give the others the good news." She started to fly off and then stopped, turning to me with an expression that was less queenly than motherly. "I have duties I can't put aside right now. My people need me. I'm counting on you to find my daughter, Naida."

I nodded. "You have my word."

I left Lea to see to the preparations of the greenhouse. She assured me she'd set a Fae sigil into the warding when it was ready. The sigil would lead Sindra's people to their new temporary home. A magical homing beacon.

I had other work to do and it looked like I'd be doing it alone. That thought didn't fill me with as much despair as it should have.

I had an idea.

Turning to my friend, I said six words I never dreamed I'd say to anyone. "I need to borrow your frog."

Lea narrowed her gaze on me. She looked, for a moment, as if she would argue, but something in my expression must have warned her off. She nodded instead. "Come with me to the greenhouse. He's in the pond."

I frowned. "I didn't know you had a pond in the greenhouse." It was good news — one less thing for Lea to do before the Fairies could be called home.

"It's new. I created it just for Wally."

I fought to keep a straight face. "Wally?"

Lea grinned. "My frog. The name just came to me. Isn't it great?"

I really didn't want to comment on what it was, so I settled for a nod.

The greenhouse all but filled an entire empty lot behind Lea's shop, *Herbal Remedies with Mystical Properties*. She'd purchased the empty lot for almost nothing when she acquired her current shop. The lot was a virtual island, with zero street access. Buildings had been constructed all around it. When the planning had been done for our street, the space had been slated as a parking lot for Croakies. At the last moment, the owner of Croakies, an ancient sorcerer named Bandy Joe Barrows, had told the city he no longer wanted to purchase the lot.

It had been a dirty trick on his part. The acreage

was basically landlocked at that point. The only access was an alley between Lea's shop and Croakies, and nobody wanted to pay the exorbitant rates Bandy Joe was going to charge to get to it.

Not to mention there would be no visibility for the location.

The end result is that Bandy Joe created a magical buffer which came in very handy when the KoA in place had to deal with a particularly... rambunctious...magical artifact.

For example, there'd been a pink elephant once. Her name had been Rosalynn. I'd had to house her in the lot for a full two weeks because she refused to enter the artifact library.

Fortunately, for Sebille and me, people tended to ignore pink elephants. Therefore, nobody on the street seemed to notice there was one living right under their noses, trumpeting, rolling a giant pink ball around, and pooping mountains they could have skied down.

When Lea bought Herbal Remedies, she'd also purchased the orphaned lot, and had added the enormous greenhouse so she could grow her own stock.

I loved visiting Lea's greenhouse. No matter the weather outside, the temperature inside was always a constant seventy-four degrees. She'd also created a magical weather system that provided occasional rain, constant daytime sunlight, and an insect ecosystem, which allowed only insects that supported plant growth and health and repelled scavenger bugs.

I stopped just inside the door, closing my eyes and inhaling deeply. The combined scent of flowers and herbs was a balm to my frazzled psyche and I just wanted to take a moment to savor it.

"He's probably in the pond," Lea told me. "Back here."

I reluctantly gave up my moment of peace and followed her to the back of the large greenhouse. Like the artifact library, Lea had created a space that was twice as large inside as it was on the outside.

One of my favorite spells.

We hadn't even reached the pond before I heard Wally's throaty bellow.

"Bawump, bawump," he said in greeting.

Lea stopped in front of a Rosemary patch and smiled down at the pair of bulging eyes riding the surface of the pond. As we stared at him, Wally rose just high enough out of the water to bellow again. "Bawump."

Lea glanced my way. "Do you want me to get him?"

I fought feelings of inadequacy. I was a third level sorceress, for goddess sake. I should be able to square my broad shoulders and step up to frog handling. But I was nothing if not self-aware. It had been all I could do to handle Mr. Slimy when I'd had to do it.

Handling a wet bullfrog that was probably slimy from the water would no doubt send me screaming out of the greenhouse, earning me a permanent sissy-girl label. "Would you?"

She eyed me carefully but apparently decided not to rib me. It was the kind of thing that made me love Lea above all my friends.

Well, that, and she had this awesome greenhouse.

Lea moved to the edge of the pond and picked up a small, plastic basket I hadn't noticed before. It was filled with holes and had a lid she could close over the top.

She wiggled her fingers over the pond and said a few words in Latin that I would have recognized if I'd paid as much attention to my Latin courses as I had my magical manipulation class.

What can I tell you? Mag Man is so much more fun.

The water in the pond rose up in a column underneath the frog, draining away to leave him exposed and sitting on a pedestal of clear, blue water.

Lea stepped into the pond and scooped the basket underneath Wally, closing the lid before he could hop back out.

As soon as she stepped from the pond, flip-flops

squeaking from the water and the hem of her long skirt dripping, the water splashed back down to fill the curvy perimeter of the pool.

She handed me the basket. It was surprisingly heavy. I barely resisted a fat joke, realizing that my posterior region had grown an inch or two as the age of thirty stalked closer. I had zero room to talk.

Or room in my jeans for that matter.

"Thanks," I told Lea. "I'll try to have him back in an hour."

She nodded. "No worries. I have lots to do today."

Like save an entire race of supernormals, for example.

I went over my plan as I headed back to the shop, Wally proclaiming his displeasure with his new accommodations the entire way.

I'd use Rustin's Book of Blank Pages again, finding the clock tower page and sending Wally through it. I'd follow him inside and, with any luck, the true essence of Wally, or whatever his real name was, would greet me there.

Then it was a simple matter of asking him questions about how he'd become a bullfrog.

If I was very lucky, Wally would be more willing to talk and I could learn more about the artifact and the spell the Quillerans had used. Maybe he could even describe the place where they'd performed the ritual.

It wasn't until I stepped through the door into the artifact library that I realized there was a big flaw in my plan.

I no longer had access to the Book of Blank Pages.

14

CHAOS BY THE BOOK

I sat on my bed, staring at the basket containing the singing frog that didn't actually sing. Wally had been suspiciously quiet since we'd entered Croakies. I wondered if he needed to be put into some water or something.

I was definitely keeping my teacup away from him.

Just in case.

In that moment, I would have done anything to have Sebille back. I could really use her help figuring out what to do next. Without the Book of Blank Pages, I had no plan left. I frowned.

Or did I?

Croakies had been home base for Keepers of the Artifacts for decades. Maybe even longer. I couldn't believe none of my predecessors had a helpful book.

The Book of Blank Pages might have been a gift from Rustin, but it had taken to me like Wally to water.

Could it be the only book of its kind? I wished I'd asked Rustin more questions about the book when I'd had the chance. Questions such as, where he'd gotten it, how long he'd had it, and where it had come from.

Maybe there was another magical book in the inventory downstairs. I perked up at the thought. But I realized that, even if I had one somewhere in the building, I'd never find it in time. My artifact seeking power wouldn't work in a massive space filled with thousands of artifacts.

Sebille's, Rustin's and even Wally's fates depended on my finding it fast.

I sat in a gloomy fog for several moments, wondering how much time I had left to get back to the Quillerans.

Then I realized that it didn't matter. No matter what happened over the next few hours, I wouldn't... couldn't...give those poor kittens back to the evil witch family.

My only hope was to find a way to defeat the Quillerans, save Sebille, and return Rustin and Wally's essences to them before it was too late for them to return.

If it wasn't already too late.

It all came back to the book.

I needed it.

Inspiration struck. I jumped off the bed and headed down the stairs.

When I arrived in the artifact library, I saw that Mr. Wicked was way ahead of me. He was sitting on Shakespeare's desk, bathing a paw and waiting for me to come to my senses.

I hurried over, mumbling under my breath. "I really wish cats could talk. It would make my life so much easier." I tugged the chair close and dropped into it. I'd barely rolled myself forward before a firm pinch tweaked the cheeks of my derriere.

I leaped out of Casanova's chair with a squeal of alarm.

The arms of the chair did a happy dance as I glared down at it. "Stupid chair."

I grabbed a different chair and tugged it to the desk, dropping into it and waiting a beat to make sure I wasn't molested. When no psyche-scarring events occurred, I leaned over the desk, placing my palms over the ancient leather blotter in the center.

The aged, tooled leather had been created to look like a book, with Shakespeare's family sigil in the center of what would be the front cover, and the family motto in blurred gold letters along the spine. *Non Sanz Droict.* Not without Right.

Fortunately, as the current KoA, I had the right to utilize the magic in the desk to find a book.

I started with the obvious...or, what would have been obvious if I'd been thinking straight, and asked for a book about a tea infuser that stole a person's essence. The blotter warmed and shifted underneath my hands, the surface bubbling as if it were working out the problem.

Then a flash of light occurred above the blotter and a slim volume entitled, *Soul Magic and Other Untoward Things*, appeared, settling gently onto the scarred leather surface.

I ran my hand over the book, smiling.

The blotter shifted once more. Then cooled beneath my touch.

"Oh no, you don't. I'm not done with you."

I moved the Soul Magic book off the blotter and placed my hands palms down on the blotter again. "I need a guide book for artifact keepers."

The blotter hardly even needed to shift through its options before another flash lit the air in front of my face and a large paperback with a bright yellow and black cover sifted down.

"Artifact Keeping for Dummies," I read. I glared at the blotter. "Very funny."

The blotter lifted off the desk and went vertical, doing a happy dance on the air.

"Try to focus, now," I told the blotter. "I'm looking for a book that has no words on the pages. A book which finds what I need when I need it. Even if I don't know I need it."

The blotter went very still for a beat. Then it slammed down onto the desk. Hard. I jerked my hands back just in time to keep my fingers from being smashed underneath it.

"Temper much?" I mumbled.

But the magic-infused blotter had already begun its search. It was shifting and bubbling away, the leather scorching hot against my skin.

The artifact's version of a flashing cursor continued until I thought it was stuck. I wondered if I'd need to magically reboot the thing.

Instead, I decided to wait it out. My attention was drawn to the Soul Magic book. With mixed emotions of excitement and dread, I opened the book.

I gasped and dropped it, shoving my chair back as the face on the very first page seemed to rise above the page.

He turned bright black eyes in my direction and smiled, his expression more than a little weird and scary. I read the inscription underneath the photo, seeing that it was a picture of Doctor Mortimus Osvald, Professor of Devilry at the New York Institute of Magic.

I couldn't decide if he looked evil or insane.

Maybe both?

I quickly turned the page but, unfortunately, the mad doctor appeared on that page too. He turned his head to look at the contents of the page. His scraggly dark brown hair hung past compact ears and clung to his heavily veined neck. His skin was ruddy, rough-looking, as if someone had scoured it regularly with sandpaper to rough it up. His lips were full, cracked and dry, and his black eyes seemed to follow me no matter how I moved.

He smiled, the action lowering thick black brows over his eyes to make him look malicious. To my shock, the cracked lips began to move. "Welcome to my in-depth study of the soul magics."

I yelped, jumping out of my chair and taking a few steps backward. The black gaze followed my movement, one thick brow arching in judgment.

Apparently deciding to ignore my reaction, the head continued as if I hadn't run away screaming. "Is there a particular area of interest? Or shall we start at the beginning and work our way through the material?"

I swallowed hard, staring at the book as my brain struggled to understand what I was seeing. It was discombobulating to know that I could still be caught off guard by magic. It was also humbling.

Doctor Osvald appeared to be waiting for me to respond. I cleared my throat and finally said, "Essence stealing artifacts?"

He gave a slight nod, and the pages of the book started flickering.

I glanced toward the blotter while I waited. It was still bubbling and shifting. Please goddess it wasn't locked up. If I had to reboot the thing, it would take forever.

"Ah, here we are. A toothbrush that removes enamel on the canines and toothpaste that draws the essence out and locks it in the tube. "

"No," I said, possibly more abrupt than I should have been.

Osvald's other brow lifted and his lips twisted with unhappiness. "Onward, then."

The pages flickered again. After a moment, they stopped. "Pantaloons that pull the essence from the crot..."

"No!"

He frowned.

Pages flickered.

"This one, then. A girdle that squeezes the essence..."

"Not surprising, but, no."

When his black eyes flashed, I added, "But thanks..." in a weak voice.

More flickering pages. He sighed. "Last one." He glared my way. "Hopefully it will meet your...very persnickety...needs."

I made a small noise as an object appeared on the front page of the chapter he indicated. It was bowl-shaped and covered by a domed lid. The object was formed of silver, with a short chain protruding from the lid. The base of the bowl was perforated with a few dozen tiny holes.

"That's it!" I exclaimed.

Osvald nodded, looking pleased with himself.

"Would you prefer to read what is contained with in this text? Or take the information verbally from me, rich with the additional information contained in the footnotes provided here?"

I *preferred* to read the book and not deal with Doctor Osvald's scary face anymore. But I knew talking to him would be both faster and more informative. Given that logic, I reluctantly shoved resistance aside and nodded. "From you please." I lowered my head to hide my grimace as I said it.

"Excellent."

I glanced up to find Osvald grinning widely, his terrifying eyebrows like slashes above the glittering black gaze. "This artifact is of particular interest to me. It belonged to a dear friend who'd created it by sheer accident. Eglund Balthire collected tea infusers. He kept hundreds of them in his London home for a century. Until he was murdered just short of midnight on a foggy late spring evening and the artifact was stolen..."

"Why did he create an essence-sucking artifact in the first place?" I asked, interrupting.

Osvald glared over at me for a moment and then went on as if I hadn't spoken. "The infuser had been in his possession at the time, in a specially created box that held a particular essence which had been extracted. He'd spent a decade creating that box, knowing that having an essence in his possession was a delicate and overwhelming responsibility..."

"Then why did he remove someone's essence in the first place?" I asked, hoping he'd stop ignoring me if he realized I wasn't going to go away.

"...but his care in protecting the essence was for naught. The Société of Dire Magic had been monitoring him, unbeknownst to poor Eglund. I'd heard a rumor at the time that they had a black purpose in mind for the infuser and they intended to get hold of it by whatever means necessary." Osvald sighed unhappily. "He was on his way to me, having implored me for weeks to help him hide the device, when he was attacked and killed. He'd had the box in his possession at the time." Osvald turned a deliberate gaze on me. "The box contained the essence of a young woman who'd died of a wasting disease and had requested that Eglund put her essence into a cousin whose body was sound but whose mind had long ago fractured beyond repair."

Well, it had taken much longer than I'd hoped, but at least that answered my question. "Was he killed underneath a clock tower?"

Osvald blinked in surprise. "Why, yes. He was. I see someone's been doing her homework."

I barely kept from rolling my eyes. "The Société of Dire Magic got the infuser?"

"Unfortunately, yes."

"And the young woman whose essence was in the box?" I asked, almost afraid to know.

"Unknown, I'm afraid. Though I do know who ended up with the infuser."

I started to ask him to clarify, silly me, but he was already winding up to tell me.

"He didn't even attempt to hide it, I'm afraid. Though possession of the item was all but an admission of his guilt in poor Eglund's murder. Having power and wealth was as much a buffer against punishment then as it is today." Osvald shook his head.

I opened my mouth again but didn't get a chance to ask.

"Alcott Quilleran."

I snapped my lips closed. "Jacob Quilleran's great, great, great grandfather?"

"Yes. The story goes that he wanted the item for himself, to inject himself into a younger, healthier body. However, my understanding is that, without Eglund's hard-won expertise on the method, the experiment went very badly. I believe the family put the artifact in mothballs after his death."

"I'm guessing you can't tell me how they finally managed to make it work?"

Osvald's head shifted from side to side. "It does not surprise me that they tried again. That kind of power is irresistible to such as the Quillerans. However, they would be aware of the extreme danger involved and would no doubt have a plan for extensive losses in trying to make it work."

Yeah, I thought, I knew of at least two potential losses already. I had a thought. "Did Eglund document his method anywhere?"

"Eglund was an emotional creature. He led with his heart in all things. As a scientist, he often gave himself a tough row to hoe with his emotional decisions. But if he had left documentation behind, I truly believe he would have determined its location through an exercise of the heart."

I waited for him to expound on that, but Osvald only winked and disappeared into the book with a soft popping sound.

I swore softly and it came out as a *bleep*. Apparently, I'd spent too much time around SB. His magical curse cuffs had temporarily transferred to me.

At least I hoped it was temporary. Because, as soon as I got Sebille back, I fully intended to throw curses of several kinds at the hateful Quilleran crew.

15

CALLING ITTOQQORTOORMIIT!

*M*y mind was so deep into what Doctor Osvald had told me about the artifact, that I almost forgot about my other search. Only the soft flash of light tugged me from my thoughts, and I looked up to see the book I'd been looking for settling gently to the surface of the blotter.

Things were looking up!

I hurried over and reached for the book, which, I realized as I looked down on it, was covered in a darker shade of leather, nearly black, and had the letters, KoA embossed on the front.

I'd been right! The book *had* been a keeper's tool, which added heft to the theory that Rustin got hold of his through less than savory means. I reached for the book with both hands, intending to head upstairs and grab Wally. I would put my plan immediately into action.

My hands clasped the book, and I tugged.

Nothing.

I tugged again, putting everything I had into picking it up.

The thing felt as if it weighed a hundred pounds.

I braced my foot against the desk and screamed out my effort as I tried again to lift the stubborn volume. It didn't move.

What the...?

Wiping sweat off my brow from my efforts, I thought about the problem for a moment. Maybe it needed keeper magic so it would recognize me.

That was probably it.

I wrapped my fingers around the book again and pulled a thread of energy forward, releasing it slowly into the volume. The leather warmed and I smiled. "Gotcha."

Power blasted from the book in a violent purple wave, yanking me off my feet and sending me flying across the room. I slammed into Casanova's chair and toppled backward, hitting my head hard on the floor and knocking the breath from my lungs.

I lay there for a moment, seeing stars and feeling a bit dazed.

A magical touch slipped over my hip and caressed my left buttock. I jumped to my feet and glared at the pervy chair. "Keep your arms to yourself, you oversexed collection of wood and velvet."

The chair bounced against the floor a few times as if giggling hysterically, and then shot upright, settling back onto the floor with a final rolling bounce that seemed even lewder than usual.

I shuddered violently. Maybe if I locked it in the toxic magic room...

With that happy thought, I returned to the desk, looking down at the cranky book. "What's your deal, anyway? Your cover clearly says, KoA. I'm a keeper of artifacts. You work for me."

To my vast surprise, the book shot open and I looked down at the first page, where a gold stamp read, "Property of Alice Parker."

Of course! The KoA before me. Alice had handed over the key to Croakies when she'd turned ninety-two years old. While, as a sorceress ninety-two was her half-life, Alice had declared that she wanted to see the world, explore other magical communities, and enjoy the rest of her life with her cat, Fenwald.

Aside from a serious lack of judgment in naming her cat, Alice had been eternally charming and full of fun. We'd spent a lot of time together as she turned the business over to me. Although, I was beginning to think Alice's "one foot out the door" mentality was coming back to bite me in the same place Casanova's chair seemed drawn.

She should have told me about the book and she should have released it to me before she left. Now, I had no idea where she was.

I would need to find her. And considering that she could be anywhere in the world from Motuo, Tibet to Ittoqqortoormiit, Greenland, that would be no easy task.

Mr. Wicked rubbed against my ankles, his purr rumbling through the room. I bent down and picked him up, burying my face in his soft, warm fur. A sense of being overwhelmed swept through me. I was bereft, unsure what to do next. My safe little world had turned upside down and inside out, and I had no idea how to fix it. People I cared about were in trouble and counting on me to help them.

"What am I going to do?" I whispered into Wicked's fur. He stopped purring and looked up at me, his orange eyes flashing with energy. I watched the light flare through them and frowned, knowing that even my cat had a better handle on things than I did.

I sighed. "I'm a terrible keeper."

Wicked's paw snapped out and smacked me on the side of the face. He'd included just a tiny bit of claw on the slap, enough to snap me out of my pity party. "Ow! Stop that."

He wriggled in my arms and jumped agilely to the floor. Trotting over to the stairs, he stopped and looked my way before bounding up the steps and disappearing through the door into my apartment.

Sighing, I gave the magic book one last look and then followed him up. I'd splash water on my face, grab a drink of water, and then see if my mind cleared enough to help me figure out what to do next.

I stepped into my apartment and my gaze went to the spot on the floor where Sebille's hair had been. I moved across the room and yanked open the drawer to my nightstand, looking down at the coiled ribbon of hair. I'd tied the strands with a piece of string to keep them together. Hopefully, the tied clump of silky red hair wouldn't be the only thing I had left of Sebille when the smoke cleared.

With a sigh, I closed the drawer and headed into the kitchen.

I found Mr. Wicked sitting on the table beside my laptop and my teacup from that morning.

That had been such a long time ago. It seemed like years. Looking at the teacup made me sad. I no longer had to worry about Mr. Slimy planting his squishy backside in my cup. I should have been happy about that.

But I kind of missed the bug-eyed little guy.

The frog, not the Quilleran joy-riding in his fleshy green body.

Of course I still had Wally. I looked around and didn't see him at first, until I heard a deep-throated "Bawump!" coming from the bathroom. I felt all the blood running from my face.

Please tell me he wasn't in the toilet. If he was, I might be tempted to jiggle the handle and sing the muffin mister song. No way was I reaching into the toilet...

As I approached the door, the big frog hopped out, staring at me as if he was trying to decide if I was a dinner option.

"Don't even think about it, Mister." It might be time to get Wally something more substantial to eat than flies.

My gaze slid to my computer. I had an email from Lea telling me the Fae were settled and were very excited about their new digs. That made me smile at least. I'd helped make something right for somebody.

My email dinged and I looked at the address of the message that had just dropped into my box. Mqhighjinx@enchantedhigh.edu

I frowned down at the email. I didn't know anybody who worked at the high school. Did I?

I opened it and saw a brief message that didn't tell me much.

Bleachers on FB field. 8pm. Don't tell anybody.

I
t looked like any other high school football field. The hundred yards of carefully kept green grass and the hulking form of the metal bleachers took me back to my own time at Enchanted High School. Those had been tough years for me, filled with unexpected magical leaks and inadvertent mystical explosions.

Not pretty.

But if there's one thing that defines the teenage psyche, it's resilience. That, and the ability to bury one's head so deep in the sand you poop glass sculptures until you turn twenty-one.

Since I didn't know what I was getting myself into, I brought Lea along. Yeah, I know the email told me not to tell anyone.

First of all, I don't just do what I'm told when I have no idea who's telling me. In fact, I'm kind of well known for not doing what I'm told period.

I might have a teensy-weensy issue with authority.

And, besides, I didn't *tell* her. I just showed up at her house and said, "Come on, I need you to cover my back."

Lea being Lea, she didn't even argue. She just asked if we could drive through Monster Burger on the way home. She'd been working in the greenhouse all day and hadn't had time to eat.

Monster Burger I could do. Solving *any* of my other problems, not so much. I'd given up trying to open the new KoA book after I'd been thrown across the room a few times. And I couldn't come up with any other way to find Sebille, other than going to the Quilleran's home again. As unpalatable as that option seemed, it might be the only thing left to do.

I was stuck.

Lea waited by the fence, her keen gaze locked on the bleachers and her cell phone clutched in her hand. I'd told her to call the police if anything looked even the slightest bit hinky.

My phantom emailer hadn't specified which bleachers I should come to, so I picked the home side, figuring I had a better than fifty percent chance of being right.

Sure enough, as I approached the shadow-cloaked metal structure with an eel bracelet vibrating electrical energy on my wrist for magical protection, a girl-shaped portion of the shadows separated from the rest and stepped out in front of me.

"Hi, Naida."

I swallowed the lump in my throat and breathed a sigh of relief. "Maude. What's this about? Are you okay?"

I had a sudden, dire thought that inspired me to step closer than I probably should have to the teen.

After all, she might seem kind and normal, but she *was* a Quilleran. "You're not in danger, are you?"

She wrapped her arms around herself and shook her head. "Things are getting out of control. First Rustin and now..." She gave me a hesitant look and chewed the inside of her bottom lip. "I'm really sorry about all this. I feel like it's my fault."

"Why in the world would you think that?" I asked the teen.

She shrugged. "I gave Mr. Wicked to you." She tucked a thick ribbon of wavy blonde hair behind one ear. I marveled at the color, wondering if it was real. I'd never met a Quilleran whose hair was any lighter than dark brown. "How is he, by the way?" she asked me shyly.

"He's great. Smarter than I am."

We shared a grin.

"That litter is really smart. Magically, that is." She seemed suddenly uncomfortable and I felt a jolt of regret. I'd probably created more heat for her with her family when I took the litter. "Look, I'm sorry we took the other cats. I just couldn't leave them alone in that terrible place."

She shook her head. "I'm glad you did. I should have done it a long time ago. I wasn't brave enough." She chewed her lip for another moment. "I've been watching out for them, though. Feeding them treats and playing with them."

"That's great, Maude. You're much braver than

you think. It took a lot of courage to give Wicked to me and it takes even more to go against your family and make sure they're okay."

She didn't look convinced. "Are they...safe?"

The first niggling doubt twisted through me. Was she there to try to get information about the kittens' location? I shoved the doubt away and nodded. "I can tell you that they are being well taken care of. I can't tell you where they are because I don't know. They were taken away from here for their own safety. I'm really sorry if that causes problems for you."

"No. I'm glad. I love my family, but they're not always right." She frowned. "I learned that the hard way." She fell silent and I waited a long moment for her to tell me why she'd called me there. When she didn't, I gave her a little nudge.

"You wanted to see me?"

"Yes. I know about the frogs. I think I saw the ritual that father used. I thought it might help you free Rustin if you knew how they did it."

My pulse sped hopefully. "That would help a lot, Maude. Can you describe it to me?"

A distant owl called and Maude jumped, her wide blue gaze flying in the direction of the sound. The teen's slender face paled under the light of the partial moon. "I have to go."

"Wait!" I said, moving quickly forward to grasp her wrist. "The ritual. You need to tell me."

Maude shook her head, and my chest tightened with disappointment. But she reached into the back pocket of her jeans and pulled out a cell phone, handing it to me. "I videotaped it. I couldn't get it all, but hopefully I got most of it. Send the video to your computer and then return the phone here, hide it near the center support leg under the bleachers."

She looked as if she was going to run. I grabbed her hand, stopping her. She fixed a terrified look on me.

"My friend, Sebille. Where have they taken her?"

Maude's gaze filled with regret. "I'm sorry. I can't help you with that."

Couldn't? Or wouldn't? I fought the impulse to try to force her to tell me. She'd already risked her own safety by coming to give me the video, and she seemed terrified of something in the night. "Okay. Thanks for this." I lifted the phone.

She gave me one last look. "Be careful, Naida. Father isn't messing around. And he's already given the enforcer permission to do what she needs to do to stop you."

16

A PREDATOR RISES

I watched Maude disappear back into the shadows, suddenly worried for her safety as much as mine. If the Quillerans would tear Rustin's essence from him and stuff it into a frog, what would they do to a teen who was actively working against them?

I started toward where Lea waited with mixed feelings. I was happy to have gotten information about the ritual. But I hadn't learned anything that would help Sebille.

I couldn't shake the feeling that my friend was in terrible danger. And every hour that passed increased that danger severalfold.

"Naida!" Lea suddenly screeched, running toward me with her arms outstretched. "Behind you!"

Too late, I heard the thump of immense wings on

the air above my head. I turned in time to see an enormous owl swooping down on me, massive talons curved for what could only be a deadly embrace.

I had just enough time to look into the wide, yellow gaze before the owl grasped my arms with its deadly talons, piercing my skin and sending a scream reverberating along my throat.

Despite the tearing pain, I thrashed against the predator's lethal grip, earning myself nothing except the warm rush of blood down my arms and a belly-tipping sensation of being swooped high into the air.

I kicked out, managing to catch the owl in the underbelly and gaining the satisfaction of its muffled cry of pain. The owl swooped lower, ducking its head and ripping at my middle with its razor-like curved beak.

I arched away from it, sucking in a terrified gasp. The deadly beak sank an inch into my belly, the white-hot pain pulling the breath from my lungs.

Desperate to get away, I slammed the eel bracelet into the bird's enormous body. Electric energy arced out of it, spearing into the owl and causing it to twitch and grunt in pain.

The talons around my arms loosened briefly, but almost immediately tightened again, driving even deeper into my skin.

I screamed at the new pain, kicking harder but gaining nothing except more pain.

White energy burst from the ground, slashing across the predator's wide, feathery chest and drawing an agonized scream from its down-covered throat. The talons loosened and I started to fall, giving a terrified shriek as the ground flew up at me.

Another flare of magic swept over me like a blanket, wrapping me tight and easing me to the ground.

I forced myself to jump to my feet as soon as I hit the grass, and took off running.

A beat later, the sound of enormous wings retook the dark sky behind me.

Lea fired another arrow of pure, white energy and it exploded in front of the owl, sending it backward on a rush of sizzling magic. The huge predator slammed into the bleachers with a bone-jarring clang and slid to the ground.

Lea grabbed my hand. "Hurry. It's only stunned."

I didn't argue. I let her pull me into a run as the air around us sizzled with frantic energy. I barely slowed as I reached the car, slamming my still-shaking hand against the warm metal as I skidded to a stop.

Blood coated my fingers, making it hard to grasp the handle and open the door.

Above the thundering sound of my frantically beating heart, I heard the ominous sound of wings pounding the air again.

Lea grabbed my hand. "Go! I'll slow it down. You

need to get to a safe place, Naida. Don't go back to the shop."

I shook my head. "I'm not losing another friend. We stand together, or nobody stands."

"Naida!"

I gave her my trademark belligerent look, and she expelled a rush of frustrated air. "You don't, by any chance have that book with you, do you?"

My stomach twisted with regret. "I wish. I think Rustin took it with him."

Her lips twisted. "Leave it to a Quilleran to take back a gift."

I didn't tell her I doubted he had a choice, given the way he'd been taken. It wasn't the time for that discussion. "We need a plan to get away from this thing."

Lea wrung her hands, looking skyward. "Running is a good idea. Let's get in the car and drive. I'll keep firing at it until something slows it down."

As plans went, it was pretty sucky. But it was all we had.

I climbed inside as Lea ran around the car. Starting the engine, I stilled at the sight through my window.

The sky was shifting and sparking in the distance. The silvery moon and stars were blocked by some kind of progressing mass. It had no discernible shape, its edges changing and growing to block the night sky.

Whatever it was moved inexorably toward us from across the football field.

What looked like a thousand pinpoints of rainbow lights twinkled across the sky, undulating with movement as the pinpoints grew gradually larger.

Lea slammed the door on her side.

"What is that?" I asked her.

Lea leaned toward me to look out my window, her eyes growing wide for a beat before she smiled. "I've seen that once before." She turned to me. "When the Fae arrived at the greenhouse tonight."

I turned an awe-filled look toward the light show in the distance. "It's Queen Sindra?"

"Unless there's another Fae army around," Lea breathed.

"But how? Why?"

The airborne form of the oncoming predator briefly blocked the Fae army from view. It was getting closer by the second, and I realized we'd lost valuable time. "We need to get out of here!"

Lea nodded.

I started the car and put it into gear, only to jerk to a stop at the sound of a familiar voice.

"Naida?"

Queen Sindra? Her voice sounded so close. Like she was in the car with us. I looked at Lea and then turned to scour the back seat with my gaze.

"Naida, girl, pay attention!"

There was no mistaking the command in that voice. As my gaze swung back, it caught on a flicker of pale pink light in the rearview mirror. Sindra's delicate form, multi-hued butterfly wings gracefully cutting the air above her, was caught in the frame of the mirror. All around her, lights flickered and wove in a never-ending pageantry of seemingly delicate beauty.

But the perception of delicacy was misleading. Gram for gram, the Fae were the most powerful creatures in my wildly diverse world. "Queen Sindra..."

"Listen carefully, child. I've sent some of my soldiers ahead. They'll cloak you against the enforcer's gaze. You must flee this place. Do not go home. Find a safe place to hide, and send one of my soldiers back to tell me when you are safe so I can pull my people back. Do you understand?"

I nodded. "But why...?"

"We owe you a great debt for our new home. You and your witch. The Fae never fail to repay our debts. Besides," she said with a sad smile. "I am counting on you to find my Sebille."

My heart sank. No pressure there. But I nodded, blinking away tears. "Thank you."

She tilted her chin regally. "Stay safe, Naida Keeper. Our world would be less without you."

A whisper of sound brought our gazes upward as

a blanket of multi-colored lights spread over my small car in an opaque wash.

"The guards doing their thing?" I asked my friend.

Lea shrugged. "I'll admit I'm not really up on my Fae magic. I'll need to fix that if we survive this current mess."

Watching her watch the owl approach, I felt suddenly sad. "I'm really sorry for getting you mixed up in this."

To my surprise, she turned to me with a wide grin. "Are you kidding? This is the most excitement I've had in weeks. I'll be your wing man anytime."

I lifted my brows. "Wingman? Maybe not the best choice of words."

We both turned back to the terrifyingly enormous shape in the night sky. The owl's bulky form was backlit by the rainbow-hued army pursuing it.

As if suddenly realizing the Fae were there, the predator abruptly switched direction, turning in a wide circle as the sea of oncoming illumination adjusted and locked on.

"You must go, keeper," a masculine voice told me. I jumped in surprise, then glanced back to the rearview mirror, finding Adolfo, the guard who'd shown me through the palace earlier hovering in midair.

He inclined his chin at Lea, his handsome face flushing. "Mistress Witch."

"Hey, Adolfo," Lea said in a saccharine-sweet voice.

I spared her a glance, dancing my eyebrows before starting up the car.

"Where will we go?" Lea asked.

I thought about it for a moment. "I know I'm not supposed to go back to the shop but I can't leave Mr. Wicked and Wally alone. Once I get Wicked, I'm going to hit the road. You're going home."

"Not a chance," Lea said.

I held up a hand, shushing her. "This isn't your fight."

"It is now. The enforcer will recognize my magic signature. She'll be gunning for me as well as you."

I sighed, realizing she was right.

"Okay, but I'm not happy about it."

Strangely, however, Lea seemed to be *very* happy about it. She grinned widely.

Silly witch.

Slamming to a rocking stop in front of Croakies, I sent Adolfo and the other three guards away after thanking them for the magical camouflage.

They tried to argue but I stood firm, finally reminding them that the Queen was in a dangerous battle and needed their help.

That did the trick.

When we were alone, I looked at Lea. "Gather up anything you think you might need to do the soul spell and a few clothes. I'll grab the two critters and meet you back here in ten minutes."

She nodded and headed toward her shop.

I opened my own door and stopped, turning to yell at her. "And snacks. Lots of snacks."

Lea sent me a thumbs up without turning around.

She was such a good egg. I needed to give her something to thank her for all her help.

Maybe she'd like a nice retro velvet chair. Sure it was slightly pervy, but she might enjoy that. After all, she *said* she hadn't had a date for a while. Or maybe she'd like a bleeping parrot?

Hm, I'd have to give it some thought. After all, my gratitude knew no bounds.

And I had a lot of annoying...er...special artifacts at my beck and call.

Mr. Wicked met me at the door, his orange gaze wide and his small form vibrating with excitement. As usual, he seemed to know what we were about to do before even I did. It was humbling being around a witch-trained cat.

"I'm just going to grab a few things, Mr. Wicked. Then we need to be off." I stumbled over something on the floor and had to grab a bookshelf to keep from going down. Wicked's metal bowl rolled over the carpet and clanged noisily into the sales counter.

I eyed the small mound of Wicked's things. While I'd been sleuthing and running from giant, predatory owls, my cat had been packing all his favorite things.

And I do mean *all* of them.

I spotted a bag of catnip, his favorite laser light toy, a box of fish-flavored treats, his pillow — Side note: I have no idea how he got the pillow downstairs. I really needed to test him for latent magic soon — his favorite stuffed mouse, his food and water bowls...

"Bawump!"

His frog...

"Wally! How'd you get out of your basket?"

Wally's tongue shot out and snagged a crawling bug off the carpet. While I was glad he was eradicating my insect population, I really didn't have time to coral him again when it was time to leave. I gave Wicked a look. "It's your responsibility to make sure he gets back into his basket when it's time to go. You have five minutes."

Wicked rubbed against my leg, purring loudly as if he hadn't a care in the world.

I envied him that feline optimism.

I grabbed a suitcase out of my closet and threw a few pairs of underwear, a clean tee-shirt, some stretchy pants, and a sweatshirt inside.

The rest of the space I filled with my computer, food for Wicked and some bottles of water for Lea and me.

Then I hurried downstairs and, on an impulse, grabbed Doctor Osvald's book and shoved it inside. I stood in the artifact library, feeling as if there were a thousand things I should grab. I finally settled, reluctantly on one, okay two, artifacts that I hoped would protect us if we came up against the Quillerans.

I zipped up the bag and rolled it out to the shop, locking the connecting door and saying a quick incantation, a spell with its roots deep in KoA history. The magic would expel everyone except keepers from trying to enter the room.

I tried not to consider the instinct that told me to do that. If I didn't return, the next keeper would be the only person who could breach the magic locks.

I spared a beat to feel sorry for that person. Whoever it was, I hoped he or she didn't waste energy and frustration trying to change the name of the shop.

That way lay madness.

Wicked was sitting beside his pile in front of the door when I headed toward the exit. Wally-in-a-Basket was beside him, the lid open on his plastic basket and a protuberant black gaze peering at me over the top. Mr. Wicked looked so proud as I told him what a good boy he was. I couldn't help giving him a quick snuggle, though he squirmed impatiently in my arms.

I set him back onto his feet and scooped all of his goodies into the suitcase. "Let's go," I told my critters, scooping up the basket and opening the door for Wicked.

"Wait," I told him, stepping around the little cat and staring up and down the street before nodding for him to go outside.

Lea's door slammed shut as I was setting the special locks on the front door, adding the keeper-only ward there too.

She hurried up, her flip flops slapping against the concrete. She was rolling two enormous suitcases along behind her.

"What in the world do you have in there?" I asked, wondering if we were going to be able to fit it all inside my little car.

She shook her head. "A little of this, a little of that." She chewed her lip worriedly as she looked down on the two bags. "I hope I didn't forget anything."

Settling Wicked and Wally into the back seat, I couldn't resist teasing her. "Did you bring your bed?"

"Covered," she said without hesitation. Her eyes sparkled as I looked aghast.

I popped the trunk and we wrestled the bags into the small luggage area. "Troll snot!" I murmured, trying to get the trunk to close.

"Naida?"

My little bag kept getting stuck in the door when I tried to close it. I tugged it out and moved Lea's bags around, shoving my much smaller suitcase into the hole I'd made.

Lea's hand found my wrist. "Um, Naida?"

I slammed the trunk, rubbing the back of my hand over my brow to wipe away the sweat. "What?"

"That doesn't look good."

I followed her line of sight and barely kept from gasping. "Frog's cankles," I muttered. I jerked into motion. "We need to go!"

Lea was barely in the car when I took off, leaving behind some of the rubber on my tires as I peeled away from the curb.

Still, it took only a few moments before the massive wall of oily black smog reached us, and only a heartbeat longer for it to completely envelop my small car.

17

DANG MY AUTHORITY ISSUES!

Okay, I'll admit, my problems with doing as I was told sometimes came back to bite me in the derriere. I wish I could tell you that made a big enough impression on me to change. But, yeah, I had a lot of faults. Lying to myself wasn't one of them.

But enough about me...

"What in the name of all the gods and goddesses is that?" Lea asked. I threw on the brake as the fog enveloped us, unable to see beyond the cloaking mess to move forward.

A strange, all-encompassing silence filled the car, broken only by the odd sound of Wicked purring.

My cat was weird.

My gaze slipped over the windows, to the windshield, beyond which the roiling smog spun and drifted, covering the range of pale gray to black and something even darker, which looked like infinity in a terrifying way. "I don't know."

The car creaked softly and we yelped as it shook from side to side.

Wicked's purr filled the ominous silence.

"What's up with your cat?" Lea asked, her widely terrified gaze locked on the miasma beyond the glass.

"No clue," I said in a low monotone. I couldn't shake the feeling that the silence was necessary to keep from waking whatever beast nudged against us from outside.

Purrrrrrrrrrr

I threw a glare over my shoulder. "Shh!"

Wicked stared back at me, his gaze inscrutable.

The car creaked again. Louder than the last time. And we threw out our arms to brace ourselves as it toppled slightly sideways and seemed to go airborne. The sense that we'd left the ground was unproven since we had no way of judging our relative position against the earth, the sky, or anything in between.

We were blinded by the magic-induced smog, apparently airborne and, judging by the way we were suddenly thrown back against the seats, we were moving fast.

"I don't like this," Lea murmured, her knuckles white against the door and dashboard.

"This shouldn't have been possible," I

responded. "The Fae cloaked our car. How did the witches even find us?"

Lea shook her head and gave a startled cry as the car seemed to slow, then tipped violently sideways, jerked forward again, and made a dizzying drop that had us both caterwauling like terrified children.

The car bounced once and shimmied violently. But I got the sense we were no longer moving. We sat in silence, even Wicked's purring had finally stopped, and I listened to the sound of the blood roaring through my ears.

Terror had me firmly in its clutches. I decided in that moment that I'd rather face a hundred giant owl enforcers than spend one more second being blindly compelled by infinity in a fog.

I thought about that as the smog started to clear.

Well...maybe not a hundred enforcers. But definitely one.

Maybe.

When the fog oozed away, I expected to be sitting outside the Quilleran home we'd so recently breached.

We weren't.

In fact, we weren't *outside* of anything. We appeared to be inside a large, concrete and metal building.

Lea and I held perfectly still for a long moment, waiting for whatever nightmare the Quillerans had devised for us next.

When nothing happened, we shared a look.

Finally, I reached for the handle and opened my door. I tested the floor for firmness and then stepped out, looking around. It was clearly the inside of a warehouse building. Not an enormous building but a sturdy and relatively clean one.

There was very little light in the space. Only the silvery trails of moonlight that filtered through a row of high windows illuminated the single, large room. The place smelled slightly musty, unused, with a tinge of rodent giving the stale scent an unkempt piquancy.

We appeared to be alone.

Lea and I looked at each other over the car.

"What just happened?" I asked my friend.

She shook her head. "Maybe that was part of the fairy cloaking magic?"

"Maybe." I decided, for my own sanity, to go with that. "Well," I glanced around. "It's not a bad place to set up for now." Opening the door to the back seat, I urged Wicked to jump out. "Maybe you can scry on it and figure out where we are."

Lea nodded. "On it." She opened the trunk and started pulling out suitcases.

I leaned across the backseat and reached for Wally's basket, squealing in alarm as the leather under my bracing hand warmed and rolled. I jumped back and smacked my head against the top of the car. "Ouch!"

Lea jumped into a crouching stance, hands out and fingers splayed, silver energy spitting against her blood-red painted nails. "What!? What's wrong?"

I rubbed my head and giggled. "Nice battle stance."

She looked down to her bent and splayed legs, then quickly straightened. "You startled me."

I giggled some more and then glanced into the car. "Something moved under my hand."

A terrified squeaking in the distance told me Wicked had found the source of the rodent smell. "Don't eat the residents!" I yelled at my cat. I could almost feel his disgust even from across the wide-open space.

I shifted sideways and a ray of moonlight found the back seat. A familiar dark rectangle was sitting on the worn leather of the seat.

Just about where Wicked had been sitting.

"Drooling dog shifters..." I muttered, reaching inside.

"What is it?" Lea asked, joining me in the doorway.

"The book." Upon looking more carefully at the golden letters adorning the front, I realized it wasn't the book Rustin had given me. It was the one I hadn't been able to touch before.

As soon as I held it in my hands, the book opened and pages started flipping. To my vast surprise, it stopped on two blackened pages.

I frowned. Then I realized the pages weren't really black. They were shades of black, from pale gray to blacker than black. And the surface of the picture moved and shifted as I touched it.

I'd seen exactly the same thing only moments before.

Outside my car windows.

"Meow," Mr. Wicked said as he wound himself around my ankles.

"This is the fog that just carried us here," I said in a breathless whisper.

Lea and I looked down at my cat.

My gaze lifted slowly back to hers. "Are you thinking the same thing I'm thinking?"

"I'm not sure."

We stood in silence for a beat. Then Lea frowned. "Wicked?"

"I think so," I said. "But why could he access the book and I couldn't?"

She shrugged. "Familiar magic is more easily transferred than Keeper magic. Or any other kind of magic for that matter. I'm guessing the person who owned the book before used a feline familiar to lock it and Wicked, being especially talented, probably found a way around the magical lock."

"Huh."

Lea stared a moment longer at my kitten, and then nodded. "Well, I'll get my scrying things set up."

I nodded absently, looking from the book to my magically talented cat. "Good work, little man. I'd love to know how you got this thing to cooperate, though."

Wicked's purring response brought a grin to my lips. Maude hadn't been kidding when she'd said Wicked's litter was especially magically talented.

"Holy toad toes!" Lea exclaimed.

I looked up from the cot I was making up in the center of the space. I'd found the cots inside Lea's suitcase. After she'd pulled a square folding table from the same bag. And two chairs. And one of those water dispensers that bestows icy water which is magically delicious when you're on the run from an evil witch family.

"It's like Mary Poppins' bag!" I'd happily exclaimed as I pulled two blankets and two fluffy pillows from its depths.

"Witch, please!" Lea had said, disgusted with me. "Hollyweird totally stole that idea from me."

"What's wrong?" I asked my friend.

"Nothing's wrong, exactly. It's just...you'll never guess where we are."

I walked over to where she'd set up a wide, shallow bowl filled with Mercury, a crystal ball situated at its center.

She ran her long fingers over the ball. The silvery surface of the Mercury rippled and spun, a series of silvery funnels rising above the surface.

Inside the glass ball was a picture of the artifact library at Croakies.

I frowned. "That's impossible."

She shook her head. "My crystal doesn't lie."

"But how? Where?"

She shook her head. "You should know that better than anyone. What artifacts do you have in the room that might take us in?"

Off the top of my head, I couldn't think of anything. "This is bad. The Quillerans will find us."

She sat back in her chair. "I don't think so. Aside from the fact that you probably put special warding on the place to keep non-KoA out..."

I nodded at the unspecified question. "I did."

"And the fact that the artifacts never show themselves to non-keepers unless they're engaged."

"True..."

"And the fact that even *we* don't know where we are."

She grinned and I had to laugh too. "You make a great argument."

"We have time to figure out what's going on. Then, if I'm not mistaken, you can use that book Wicked was kind enough to bring with him to get us out of here."

She was right. On all counts. I relaxed a bit. I

hadn't wanted to worry Lea, but while she was scrying out our location, I'd opened the only door in the place and run up against a concrete block wall. No egress. In. Or out.

Soooo....

Across the room my suitcase jumped up into the air and slammed back down, angry sounds emerging through the canvas sides.

"Is that...bleeping?"

I sighed. "Yes." I'd forgotten about my security artifact. "I needed protection."

Lea stood up and followed me. "So, you brought a suitcase that swears?"

I turned to find her laughing.

"Close." I unzipped my bag and SB blasted out, shooting straight up into the air and flying a circle that included the entire width and breadth of the spacious room.

As he flew, he dropped bleep bombs like bird poop on our heads the entire time.

Clearly, he hadn't liked being packed inside a suitcase along with my spare underwear.

I reached into the bag and carefully extracted Blackbeard's sword. As I touched the hilt, the blade grew to the perfect length for my arm. My fingers felt right at home around the hilt. "I figured this might help if I needed to fight the Quillerans."

Lea nodded. "As long as you don't need to get too close to use it."

I frowned down at the blade. She had a point. A magic arrow shot a lot farther and faster than a sword could slice.

Shrugging, I decided to trust my choice. Mr. Wicked wasn't the only one who had some keen magical instincts.

My right butt cheek vibrated and I reached for my phone, only to realize it wasn't my phone.

It was Maude's. I must have slipped it into my pocket at some point when I was running from the enforcer.

The ID on the phone said only, *Pops*. I grimaced, thinking that was way too harmless-sounding for Jacob Quilleran. The witch I'd faced off against in my rooms was no *Pops*.

Needless-to-say I let the call go. A beat later, a voicemail warning showed up.

"Who was it?" Lea asked. She was squinting into her crystal, no doubt looking for clues as to where we were.

"Jacob Quilleran."

She started, her head jerking up, and I realized she thought it was *my* phone. In all the excitement, I'd forgotten to tell her about our good fortune. I held it up. "This is Maude's. She managed to tape some of the essence-stealing ritual."

Alarm faded from Lea's expressive face. "Oh, thank the goddess. Don't scare me like that."

I chuckled. "Sorry. I need to send myself the

video file." I quickly found the video and emailed it to myself. Tugging my laptop from the suitcase, I set it up on the table, sitting down across from Lea. As I opened my email, her scrying Mercury bubbled energetically. The bubbles burst in a rhythm of their own, and sent liquid metal spurting upward in random patterns, dancing to its own unheard melody.

The video email arrived with a trumpet sound that made Lea snort out a laugh. With a bleep and a flourish, SB settled down onto the table between us. "Avast ye, maidens. Guard yer bosoms."

"Don't you mean gird your loins?" Lea asked with a roll of her eyes.

I shook my head. "No. He probably means what he said. Remember, he belonged to a pirate."

"Ah, yes."

I clicked on the video to open it. Lea stood behind me, watching over my shoulder.

The scene on my screen was dark, confused, with a lot of action and shifting forms all wearing white.

I realized the Quillerans' robes were white, with blood-red scarves that hung around their necks.

"White robes? Blasphemy," Lea said.

I turned to discover her curling her lip.

"There's nothing pure about that family."

I couldn't agree more.

We watched as the be-robed forms shifted into their places around a flickering fire. The tallest participant, features obscured by a strange black mask with perky ears like a cat's, threw a handful of dust on the fire and the flames expanded on a rush of air. The orange and red of a normal flame was speared an unnatural purple by whatever the witch was flinging onto the fire.

The witch turned to someone and nodded. I got a good look at the mask in the flickering light. It *was* a cat.

Strange choice for a ritual. Movement at the bottom edge of the video caught my eye. Several small, graceful forms wove silently through the ritualists, their black coats sparking in the light of the fire as if they were covered in pixie dust.

"Are those cats?"

I nodded, pointing as the person videotaping the ritual — presumably Maude — scanned the area to pick up the four small felines circling the fire.

The witch wearing the cat mask flung another handful of dust into the fire and it flared brightly, its glow mirrored in the sigils dangling from the cats' collars.

I sat closer, squinting in an attempt to see the sigils. "Those have to be Wicked's littermates."

Lea frowned. "But they're black. I thought his litter was entirely gray, which is why the Quillerans knew they'd be exceptional magical conduits."

I threw her a quizzical look and she shrugged. "I hear things on the witch-wave."

"They *are* all black. Maybe the witches dyed them?" I shrugged. "Or it could be different cats, I guess. Though, those sigils look like the ones LA Mapes took off the kittens."

On the video, the witches around the fire all joined hands and started to chant. I couldn't understand what they were chanting, but I noticed the words had a hypnotic effect on the cats, after a few moments of chanting, the kittens stepped forward, one by one, into the fire pit.

My stomach clenched. "Oh, no, no, no."

Behind the camera, Maude gasped, and the view flew off target for a beat.

When it refocused, the cats were all standing at the edge of the fire, encircling it like the witches. The sigils hanging from their collars glowed with the eerie purple light of the fire.

Although they appeared extremely calm, maybe even hypnotized, they didn't seem to be in any danger from the fire. Instead of touching them, it danced around them, sending smoke into the air above the fire that appeared to mirror their shapes. The smoke felines had eyes the color of the fire, a deep orange, and glowed with power as they hovered above the flame.

The chanting wound down and the group fell silent.

I held my breath, unsure what would happen next, and then sucked air in a gasp as the smoke cats all plunged downward into the fire and it exploded, flame flaring out to touch everyone standing around the blaze.

It receded slowly to show that no one had been burned.

One by one the kittens stepped away and disappeared into the night, their sigils no longer glowing.

And at the center of the fire, which was only softly glowing embers at that point, sat a dull silver object shaped like a star.

The camera moved and a rock skittered past the screen. There was a soft intake of air as the masked witch's head jerked toward the person taping the event. And then the sound of scrambling and the wild thrashing of ground and sky, before everything went dark.

18

EVEN FOOLS ARE OCCASIONALLY RIGHT

I sat staring at the blank screen for a long moment, thinking. Lea shifted uncomfortably behind me, pulling me out of my thoughts.

I hit the play button and watched the video again. And then one more time.

Shaking her head, Lea returned to her scrying after the second viewing. "I just feel so bad for those kittens. They were like..."

"Zombies?" I provided, a sour taste in my mouth. "They were obviously under some kind of spell."

Lea frowned. She sat in her chair, staring at her crystal ball, clearly disturbed by what she'd seen.

She jumped when I slammed the top of my computer closed to stop myself from watching the video again. I looked across the table. "Sorry."

"It's okay. It's frustrating. I feel like all the pieces are here and we just can't put them together."

I nodded silently. "I've seen those sigils before. They were hanging from the kittens' collars."

Lea's eyes widened and she sat forward. "Do you still have them?"

"No. But LA might. Her witch was going to dig into them."

Lea tapped the table between us with a long, pink nail. "Call her. If those sigils were used to engage the infuser we're looking for, they'll have magical residue from this ritual."

I hesitated. "I don't want to be a party pooper, but I'm sure these objects have been used in lots of rituals by now."

Lea nodded. "Yes. But unless the Quillerans are using black magic on a regular basis, that won't matter. Dark magic leaves behind a sooty aura that's fairly easy to see."

I picked up my cell, quickly dialing LA. She answered on the third ring. "Naida. I'm glad you called. I was just going to call you. We need to talk."

"What's happened?" I asked my friend, surging to my feet. Adrenaline coursed through my veins.

"Deg's been testing those sigils. We think they've been used in a black magic ritual fairly recently."

I glanced at Lea. "LA, my friend Lea's here with me. Do you mind if I put this on speaker?"

"Is she a witch?"

"Yes."

"Good. Then, yes."

I hit the button and set the phone down on the table between us. "You're on speaker."

"Lea," said a deep voice that wasn't LA, "Have you ever tested Naida's kitten for black magic?"

My friend and I shared a horrified glance.

"Why are you asking?" I demanded angrily.

Deg sighed. "Stay calm, sorceress. You wanted to get to the bottom of this, right?"

I fought my impulse to argue. He was right. But I really didn't like the direction the conversation had taken. "Yes. But what does Wicked have to do with this?"

"These kittens..." Deg hesitated a moment and then seemed to gather his thoughts again enough to speak. "They're not normal cats."

I rolled my eyes.

"I saw that," Deg said smugly.

All the color left my face and Lea giggled behind her hand. "You think they were specially bred for Magicke Noire?" she asked the other witch.

"I do. And they're exceptionally gifted. I'd almost say they were better witches than most witches."

Lea looked startled. "Consciousness Infusion?"

"Maybe, but I'm almost thinking it's bigger than that."

"Bigger how?"

"Have you ever heard of Energy Entrapment?"

Lea paled. Her gaze skimmed to mine and something ugly twisted inside my belly. I lifted my hands.

"Can somebody please speak in something other than witch gibberish?"

"We believe someone's been stealing magic, probably from several magical species, and infusing it into these cats," LA said.

My knees gave out and I dropped heavily to my chair. "But I thought they were just stealing souls and transferring them into frogs."

Wicked jumped onto the table and sprawled over my computer, batting playfully at my hand as I reached to scratch his belly.

"I think that's one phase of the process," Deg said. "They need the essence because that's where the magic is stored. But they don't want the whole, human consciousness. They only want the magic. I believe they'll strip your Mr. Slimy of his magic and leave him trapped inside that frog. Eventually, even his humanity will leave him."

The dark something inside my chest flared oily and cold, making the room suddenly feel like a freezer. "But that's..."

"Horrific. Yes. I know," Deg said. "It goes against everything witches believe in. They need to be stopped."

Tears burned my eyes. Poor Rustin. Whatever he'd done, or been as a Quilleran, he didn't deserve to be forever trapped, magic-stripped, inside a slimy old frog.

My gaze slid to Wally. By all accounts, he'd been

in that form longer than Rustin and, since Lea and I'd had access to him, he hadn't shown himself to us in any other form. Had he already been stripped? The additional fact that the Quillerans had been willing to trade him for Mr. Slimy didn't bode well. He clearly had no value to them.

I suddenly wondered what type of magical creature he'd been.

"We need to help these people," Lea said. She was staring at Wally's basket across the room. Apparently, she hadn't come to the obvious conclusion. It was probably too late for poor Wally.

Then I had an even more terrifying thought. "Sebille!"

Lea flinched as if I'd struck her. "Oh, my goddess!"

"Yes, your friend is in terrible danger," LA said. "Sprite magic is particularly potent. And her royal blood gives her an extra edge. They initially might have taken her to force your hand, but they've no doubt figured out what she is by now. Even if you do whatever they ask, they won't be returning her to you. At least not in her sprite form."

Stars burst before my eyes. Rage replaced horror and fear. "How do we stop these monsters?"

"That's why I asked about your kitten," Deg said gently. "If he's been used in one of these rituals, there's a pathway in his mind we might be able to follow to find where they're keeping your friend."

I glanced down at Wicked. He had one of SB's colorful feathers between his paws and he was kicking at it with his back feet. He looked adorable.

He looked like a sweet, harmless kitten.

But I'd seen him outsmart me on several occasions. And, while outsmarting me wasn't exactly proof of stunning intellect, it was definitely a sign that he was more than he appeared.

"Will it hurt him?" I asked softly, reluctant to even go down that road.

There was the briefest hesitation. I closed my eyes, suddenly unable to breathe.

Finally, Deg said. "I just don't know. If we're very careful, hopefully not."

My head was already shaking. I just couldn't. I sat silent for a long moment and then sighed. "I'm sorry." I disconnected, knowing I was letting everyone in the magic world down by rejecting a chance to save the Quilleran's victims. But I just couldn't sacrifice Mr. Wicked to help them.

Lea and I sat silent for several moments. I could feel her indecision across the space. She wanted to ask me to do it. But I was certain she understood why I couldn't.

Finally, she said. "We'll find another way."

I nodded, knowing that was a fool's hope. But it was the only hope this fool had.

I grabbed the book from inside the car and carried it over to the table.

Lea frowned. "What are you doing?"

"The only thing I know to do at this point. I was hoping to use this to pull Wally out and question him about the ritual." My heart hurt as I realized he might no longer have the humanity to do what I needed. "I have to try." I hated that the words came out tinged in desperation.

Lea nodded but didn't say anything.

I grabbed Wally's basket and settled it on the table. Touching a page in the book, I thought about what I wanted the pages to show me. If Wicked had called for the cloaking fog earlier, then voice commands weren't necessary. I pictured the clock tower in my mind and, to my delighted surprise, the pages started to flip.

A moment later, they drifted open on the familiar depiction of the clock tower. As before, the clock read eleven forty-five pm.

I took a deep breath and reached for Wally, picking him up with two hands. Though I grimaced when my fingers touched the oversized amphibian, he didn't feel nearly as repulsive as I expected.

I was apparently getting used to handling frogs.

Disturbing.

With a happy meow, Mr. Wicked dove for the page, disappearing into the picture. I was aware of

Lea's gasp of surprise as I reached out and placed my palm over the image from the past.

As before, the magic grabbed me top and bottom and magically wrung my limp form like a wet cloth. A beat later, it ripped me out of the warehouse room and into the world depicted on the page.

My feet slammed down on the cobblestones but I kept my balance. Also like before, a thick fog swirled around me, disorienting and oppressive. I jumped when Wicked found my ankles, winding his soft warmth comfortingly around them.

The familiar rhythmic ticking of the big clock sounded like a heartbeat, reverberating through the fog until it gained a life of its own. I glanced up, seeing that the hour had already moved forward five minutes.

I didn't have much time.

I glanced around for Wally. No man-shaped shadowy forms existed in the fog with me.

It was me and Wicked, and nothing else.

No frogs or people.

I tried to remember if the frog had come through with me the last time, or if it had morphed into Rustin instead.

I remembered seeing Wicked, but I couldn't remember Mr. Slimy.

Footsteps suddenly reverberated through the fog and I tensed. Too late, I realized the folly of jumping back into the book. I had no way of knowing who might be in there with me. It could just as easily be Jacob Quilleran as poor Wally.

Wicked's head came up and he gave a hiss, but then he trotted into the fog, his tail high and the hair on his back smooth.

"Wicked! Come back here," I whispered harshly, hesitant to draw any attention to myself, just in case.

A silhouette was etched in the fog several feet away. I took a step backward, panic rising. Where was my cat?

The shadows writhed and lightened until a familiar form stepped out of the fog.

I almost forgot to breathe.

Rustin!

"How did you get here?" I asked the cursed witch.

He hurried forward, a plea in his gaze. I fought the urge to recoil. After all, I'd come to get answers and Rustin could give them to me as easily as Wally. "Where's Wally?"

Rustin frowned. "I felt the void in the spell and filled it. But my power is waning. I won't be able to come again."

Void? Was he verifying what I already suspected? Was Wally...gone?

Rustin glanced up at the face of the clock, which had moved another four minutes since he'd appeared. "We don't have much time. I need to tell you this because I doubt I'll get another chance."

"I'm listening."

He nodded, pacing away from me, wringing his hands. Mr. Wicked curled up around one of my feet and fell asleep, immersed in the fog swirling around our ankles. "I can't tell you how they performed the ritual. I was unconscious. They told me I was hit by an errant jolt of energy and knocked out. The fact that I didn't remember didn't surprise me. My head had been killing me just before my memories fled. I remember Candace giving me a cup of tea..."

My eyes widened. "You drank tea they'd infused with the artifact?"

"That was my memory. Only...I'm not sure that's right now. They might have placed that recollection in my head. I only remember a flash of light. And then a stomach twisting sensation of falling. But I never really landed. I finally opened my eyes and looked around. The world was much larger, and my view of it was distorted." He glanced at me, humiliation filling his handsome features. "And then I..." He gagged, covering his mouth with a hand. "I ate a bug."

I rolled my lips to keep from smiling. I mean, it was funny that the bug-eating was the thing that bothered him most. But I was pretty sure he wouldn't appreciate my amusement. "You were a frog?"

"Yes. And no. I was definitely in a frog's body, with a frog's instincts. But I was still me."

I made a sound of sympathy, and his jaw tightened. "I watched them carry me...my body...out of the room and tried to follow, but someone grabbed the frog and threw me into a box. I remember being carried for a while. It seemed like a long while, but I have no idea if my perspectives on time were mine, or the frog's. They shut me in a room with a small pool and lots of bugs flying around." He grimaced. "My mind..." He shook his head. "I was losing whole chunks of time to the frog. That was when I realized I needed to start forming a plan fast, before I lost myself for good."

"How did you end up at *my* house?"

He skimmed me a quick look, humor glinting in the depths of his eyes. "I found the book. Someone had left it in the room and, when I approached it, the book seemed to recognize me. It opened right up without my touching it. When the pages stopped flickering, there was a picture of Croakies."

I opened my mouth to ask more questions, specifically about why the KoA book hadn't recognized me while it had apparently recognized my cat, but he shook his head, striding closer and grasping my forearms, his gaze filled with urgency. "There's no more time for talk. I must tell you."

I nodded, realizing I couldn't stop him even if I wanted to. A quick glance upward told us both we had about a minute before we'd return to our respective worlds.

"There's a way to fix everything. But you must listen carefully. The Enforcer is the key. The soul magic was her idea. She loves tea and visits the tea shop down the street every morning for her special blend. She's too strong to defeat in the usual way, but her ego is her weak spot. She doesn't take precautions because she believes she's invincible. You need to use that against her."

Gong.

The first stroke of midnight throbbed high above our heads, the sonorous tone reverberating through the fog and vibrating beneath my feet.

Rustin's grip on my arms increased to the point of pain. "You must convince her she's been transformed into something that would weaken and terrify her."

Gong.

His hands trembled against my skin. "Once she believes she's been transformed, convince her you'll make sure she loses herself to that form if she doesn't help you find where they're keeping me and tell you how to return me to my body."

Gong.

Sweat broke out on his smooth brow. "She knows how to reverse the spell."

Gong.

"The Enforcer is the key."

Gong.

"But how will we convince her that her essence has been stolen?" I asked.

Gong

"You won't. She knows the artifact is safe wherever they've hidden it. You have to convince her that you've changed her form completely."

Gong

I frowned. "What's the difference?"

Gong

"There's no time to explain. Ask your friend the witch."

Gong

"But..."

The fog lifted from the ground, quickly consuming Rustin's tall form.

Gong

His gaze blazed with intensity and fear. "You must do this, Keeper of the Artifacts or the artifact and I will be lost forever."

Gong

The fog rose above his neck, obscuring all but his blazing eyes. When he spoke again, his voice burned an imprint in my mind. *I'm counting on you, Naida.*

Gong

All the air left the space where I stood. The fog surged upward, bathing me in moist chill. At my feet, Wicked stirred. I panicked. What would happen if I wasn't holding onto him when the magic grabbed me? Would Wicked be left behind?

With a desperate cry, I bent double, immersing myself in the fog. I'd barely gotten hold of his tiny, soft body before the magic grabbed hold, twisting me like laundry on a wind-battered clothesline.

Pain razored through my body. My mouth opened on a silent scream. And the world around me was ripped away. Only the last, mournful reverberations of the final gong were left sifting through my mind.

19

AVAST! YE COCKROACH YE

When I landed back in the hidden warehouse room, Lea was pacing around the table, holding the book. Her knuckles were white against the dark leather. She gave a relieved cry as she saw us, running over and grabbing me into a hug. Lea's desperation earned her an alarmed hiss from Wicked. "I was terrified. As soon as you left, the book slammed shut so hard I thought it was an evil portent of what had happened."

I waved off her concerns. "I have a plan."

She let me go, much to Wicked's relief. With an impatient yowl, he jumped from my arms and stalked away, tail snapping with irritation. "Wally was there?" My friend looked so hopeful it made me sad. "No. I'm really afraid it's too late for poor Wally."

She sighed, nodding. "I have the same feeling." We both glanced toward the basket on the table, frowning. "He didn't come back with you? Is that normal?"

I shook my head. "I have no idea what's normal in this mess. Hopefully, he'll show up. Rustin always seemed to pop up where I least expected." I realized I was speaking about the witch in the past tense, and that made me sad too.

But I shoved the energy-sapping emotion aside and quickly outlined Rustin's idea to Lea.

Her expressions ran the gamut from shocked to dubious to carefully neutral. I was afraid she was going to tell me that it couldn't be done. I frantically searched my mind for arguments to counter her expected resistance.

She was silent for a long moment when I'd finished. I chewed my lip and forced myself to wait. Lea was a very deliberative witch. She didn't do much of anything on impulse. The scenario I'd outlined for her would take some careful thought. I didn't know if a spell even existed that would make it work.

Finally, she lifted her gaze to mine. I saw sadness there and my stomach twisted. But her words belied her gaze. "It can be done..."

I narrowed my eyes. "Then why do you sound as if someone just pooped in your cornflakes?"

She grimaced, whether from my fecal metaphor or her own reservations I had no clue. "It's very complex. So many factors and facets."

"Is there a spell? Or would you have to create one?"

She shook her head. "Contrary to human fairy-tales, witches can't turn people into bugs and other things. But suggestion is a powerful thing, and we *can* create something called a four-dimensional glamour that looks and feels real enough to fool even the person who's been spelled."

I nodded, optimism a slight but tentative sweetness in my mouth.

"We're going to need help. Lots of it," Lea said, frowning.

"Just tell me what you need."

She thought for a moment. "How soon do we need to get this pulled together?"

"Tonight. Sebille's in danger. And after the appearance of the waning moon, Rustin remains permanently as a frog." Despite Rustin's urgent plea to save him from turning into a frog, I fully intended to find out about Sebille before I even broached the subject of Rustin with Margot. My priorities hadn't shifted.

Lea paled. "Well, that's definitely a challenging timeline." She shook her head. "But it can be done." She turned to my computer, dropping into the chair in front of it and wiggling her fingers to open a *Notes* application. She traced her finger quickly over the document on the screen, making a list with her energy. "You pull this stuff together while I start planning the magic involved."

Mythic Specialty Teas was owned by a local sorceress named Alissia Gibbon. Alissia seemed a harmless enough woman. Like all sorceresses, her abilities were mostly limited to her magic legacy. In her case, on her enchanted tea blends. Like me, she was very limited in the magic she could do outside her legacy, so learning that we intended to take on a powerful witch, Alissia had been understandably reluctant. It had taken some serious discussion to get her to cooperate on our sting.

Especially when she'd heard that the Quillerans and their daunting enforcer were involved.

But, when she learned what the witch family had been up to, she reluctantly agreed.

I gave her a friendly wave when we were all in place and received a tight, worried expression in return.

I glanced at Lea. "I hope Alissia doesn't give us away with her sour puss."

Lea turned from the table in the corner, where she'd been giving last-minute instructions to the undercover "customers" and threw the sour-faced proprietress a glance, sighing. "I don't have enough mojo to glamour her. There are just too many moving parts in this."

I nodded. "We'll just hope for the best then." I didn't want to burden Lea with anything more. She definitely had her hands full.

But I wasn't one to let Fate take the reins if there was another option. I moved through the crowded tea shop, my nose twitching under the delightful aromas of Alissia's teas. As I approached, the woman seemed to get even more tense, her pale-blue gaze becoming even more worried.

"Hi, Alissia." I leaned on the counter, giving her a smile.

To my shock, she smiled back. "Naida. How's it going?"

The way she asked the question made it clear she was asking about our orchestrated sting, rather than life in general.

"It's going all right. But I'm worried you're not up to lying to Margot. This is going to be a whole lot more dangerous on everyone involved if she notices anything different about you."

Alissia stared hard at me for a long moment, as if she were going to take exception to my charge, but then her face broke into a wide grin, transforming her from almost plain-looking to truly beautiful. A golden aura shone from her newly bright blue eyes and the sweet scent of lavender wafted away from her.

She seemed to be waiting for me to understand something. I shook my head. "What am I missing?"

"This is the real me," Alissia said with obvious delight. She let the grin fade and the aura turned to ash, drifting toward the floor. "This is what my clients see. This is what the enforcer will expect. I use a glamour every day in the shop."

Aside from my respect for the phenomenal amount of energy that must take, I was curious. "Why would you do that?"

Alissia gave me a sly look, her gaze sparkling. "I have my reasons. But, trust me, Margot expects to see a sour-faced, terrified woman when she comes into Mythic Teas. And that is exactly what she'll see." She touched my hand. "I've got this. The Quillerans have harmed everyone and everything they've ever touched. It's time for them to pay for at least one of their actions."

Warmth spread through my chest and tears filled my eyes as I thought of Sebille. I hoped she was still all right.

"Showtime!" yelled a bright, obviously amplified voice from the front door. I glanced around to see a familiar, tiny form hovering before the door. As I caught his eye, Adolfo saluted jauntily and shot off down the street to watch the target approach.

I took a deep breath and squared my shoulders, giving Lea a reluctant glance as I clutched the massive orange pill in my hand.

She nodded, smiling her encouragement.

I had to push the pill to my lips with both hands but, despite my bone-deep reluctance, I managed to stuff it into my mouth.

Still, it took Alissia's gentle touch on my shoulder to get me to chew and swallow. I was all too cognizant of SB's contribution to the foundations of the magic pill.

I felt the first jolt of the changes as Margot moved into view on the other side of the large, front windows.

By the time she'd pulled open the door, I was perched on Lea's shoulder, looking down on the surprising visage of an old man with copious white hair sticking out of his ears and nose.

Ugh! When Lea did a glamour, she really went all out.

Margot entered the shop with a confident stride, her sleek black hair blowing softly in the air from the vent above the door. She skimmed a look over the tables and the dozen or so people sipping and chatting, seemingly oblivious to her arrival.

I danced back and forth on Lea's shoulder, cocking my head to adjust to the extra layers of UV light and vibrant colors I could see in my current form. For a moment, I got distracted by my newfound ability to focus on Margot while still reading the gold lettering on one window, as well as the poster depicting the different herbs on the other window.

Being a bird was the Gargoyle's Sneakers.

Visually speaking at least.

There was no way I was eating worms or bugs.

Did parrots even eat bugs?

As Margot's hostile gaze landed on me, I lifted my wings and danced to the side as I'd seen SB do a hundred times. I opened my beak and, before I could stop myself, I said, "Hello, my pretty. Polly want a cracker?"

The Enforcer's hostile gaze narrowed for a beat, probably remembering her dubious experience with SB at my house, and then skimmed downward to take in the old guy whose shoulder I was perched on.

Lea lifted her tea with thick, gnarled fingers and took a sip. She turned a "get off my lawn" expression to Margot and the glare seemed to be enough to relax any reservations the Enforcer had about the parrot in the room.

Margot headed toward the counter to order her tea. As agreed, Alissia filled an infuser with a slightly doctored loose tea and poured boiling water over it in a small pot. She grabbed a bran and raisin muffin from the display case, and placed everything on a small, wooden tray. She fixed her pale, worried gaze on Margot. "Have a nice day."

Margot seemed to hesitate. She stared for a long

moment at Alissia and I saw the other woman tense. I nervously pranced across Lea's shoulder, inadvertently scratching her on the ear with one of my claws.

She reached up and flicked me with a finger. I flew into the air, squawking and beating my wings with indignation.

Margot turned around and grinned as she saw me land on the woman at the next table, my claws getting caught in her poufy, gray-brown hair. The woman grunted in outrage. "Hey! Mister, keep your stupid bird under control."

Lea sipped her tea and ignored everything.

The woman stood up and, shoving at her hair, walked over to point a finger into Lea's grizzled face. "Did you hear me?"

Lea seemed to startle, her head coming up, and she held a gnarled hand behind one ear. "Eh? What did you say, lady?"

Margot grinned widely, enjoying the show. She dropped into an empty table in the back corner and poured herself some tea as the poufy-haired woman swung an arm in my direction. I took to the air, flying in frantic circles and squawking, "Parrot abuse, parrot abuse! Bwawk!!"

I flew right at Margot, causing her to duck her head.

While her head was down, I released the small bundle of herbs and fairy dust Lea had given me.

The sachet opened above Margot's head, sending its contents wafting down on her.

Lea threw up a hand and a fine, iridescent blue dust filled the air, sifting outward to travel through the entire room.

"Watch out, you stupid bird or I'll roast you for dinner," Margot growled.

I flew away, happy to avoid that fate in whatever form I was in. I landed on the counter and waited for the tea to take effect.

Margot blinked rapidly and then shuddered.

The proprietress engaged the next phase of her role. "Hey, you. Old man. Get this bird out of my shop." Alissia yelled across the room.

Lea grabbed the cane she'd left leaning against the table and slowly stood, her bones creaking with the effort.

I had to remember to congratulate her later on her excellent subterfuge.

She lifted an arm and I flew over to land on it. But instead of heading for the exit, we headed for the restrooms at the back of the shop. A path that would take us directly past Margot's table.

Margot shuddered again and then doubled over as a long, loud gurgling noise erupted from her middle. She groaned loudly.

As we passed her table, Lea suddenly straightened and, lifting a hand, flung a handful of pixie magic over the enforcer with a muttered command.

"*Adtenuo!*"

Margot's head shot up, her mouth came open on a long, drawn-out hiss and she fell from her chair, hitting the floor as she disappeared in a shower of sparks.

The shop was silent, expectation hanging in the air like the remaining dust.

Everyone stared at the small, dark oval on the floor and then Lea's gaze found the two women at the nearby table. The first one, a young woman with long, straight blonde hair she had pulled back in a high ponytail, surged from her chair, her gaze locked on the spot where Margot lay. She screamed. "Cockroach!" Her throat muscles contracted under the primal scream and she scurried back, knocking over chairs and spilling cups of tea in her hurry to vacate the shop. The woman who'd been sitting at the table with her tried to stomp on Margot, her thin lips twisting with revulsion. "Disgusting creature!"

Lea eased sideways, pushing the woman back with her drooping, old guy shoulder. "Step back, everybody. I've got this," she said in a deep, rusty voice. Lea lifted her cane in the air and slammed it down mere inches from Margot's cockroach-clad body.

The bug finally shook off its stasis and scurried away, heading for a hole in the molding behind the nearest table.

With a smile, Lea dropped her glamour and

lifted her hand, energy sizzling against her palm. She threw the energy toward the bug. "*Desino!*"

Margot stopped mid scrabble and stood there twitching as if trying to throw off Lea's magic. It was one of the things we'd been most worried about when we'd come up with our plan. The Enforcer was a powerful witch in her own right. It was entirely possible she'd find a way to overthrow Lea's magical shenanigans.

Which was why we needed to move fast.

I swooped down and landed next to the cockroach. My inner disgust meter was clanging wildly as I forced myself to grab the bug with my beak.

I nearly spat her back out. The feeling of those revolting little legs wriggling against my lips...er... beak was enough to make me gag.

Lea grabbed the book she'd been pretending to read and held it out, showing me the clocktower page I'd settled into place earlier. I flapped my wings and flew toward the book, anxious to spit out my prisoner.

It was almost a relief when my talons hit the page, to feel the magic twisting against me, tugging the nasty bug from between my lips.

At the last, possible moment, I felt Lea's hand wrapping around one of my wings and felt the vibration of her surprised scream as the magic yanked her inside the book with me.

20

A MYSTERY SOLVED

*L*ea and I landed in a tangle of legs and arms, hitting the slimy cobblestones and skidding sideways. I was vaguely aware of the sound of a heavy body hitting the stones and the muffled sound of swearing that was softened by the fog.

Keeping her hand on my shoulder, Lea glanced toward the clock face. As usual, it was set for eleven forty-five. At the top of the hour, we'd all be sent on our merry way.

That was all the time I had to convince Margot that she was going to stay a bug forever unless she helped us.

Seeing the rage contorting her face as she stood and turned to face us, I was thinking I might not live for the full fifteen minutes.

"I wouldn't, if I were you," Lea said, her hand still

warm on my shoulder as we stood. "If you kill us, you'll be stuck as a cockroach for the rest of your miserable life."

Margot's big hands were fisted at her sides, her face purple with rage. "How dare you! Do you have any idea what you're dealing with, witch?"

Lea shrugged. "Actually, I do. I'm dealing with a witch who's now a cockroach."

I was impressed by her calm demeanor. Personally, I was thinking I should have worn a water barrier on the outside of my panties.

If I wet myself, I'd never live it down.

Margot growled, flinging her hands up and screaming something in Latin.

Okay, I'll admit I don't know as much Latin as I should. I was pretty good at deciphering it in written form. But the spoken language made my eyes cross.

Whatever the command was, it fell into the fog and died, unrealized. Margot stared at her hands, looking confused.

"You probably aren't aware of the Blattarium Episodium," Lea said in an offhand way. "It's a special group of transformation magics only Sprites can conjure. Unfortunately for you, when Queen Sindra learned you'd taken her daughter, she was only too happy to help us take you down."

Margot's wide face lost some of its belligerence. I didn't know if there was such a thing as a Blattarium

Episodium, but all that was important was that Margot seemed to believe it.

"I'll kill you all for this!"

Lea simply stared back at the other witch until Margot's rage fizzled out, leaving behind only fear. "What do you want?"

I glanced nervously at the clock. It had moved eight ticks since we'd landed there. Not much time left.

Already the fog was becoming more agitated.

"We want the location where the Quillerans are keeping Princess Sebille..." Lea let the name sink in for a moment, reminding Margot that she was playing with fire herself by abducting the Fae princess. "And we want the artifact you're using to steal people's essence."

Margot stared at us for a long beat as the moments ticked loudly by overhead.

"You have just under four minutes," I reminded the witch, earning a growl for my troubles.

A minute later, I said, "three minutes."

"All right. The princess is in a special room below the ground."

"Where, below the ground?" I barked out, losing patience. "You know, you're the only one who'll still be a cockroach when this is over if you don't cooperate."

"Under the cat house," Margot growled out, her fists clenched.

"And the artifact?" I asked.

Gong!

Margot looked at her feet.

Gong!

She clenched her jaw.

Gong!

"I can't give you that..."

Gong!

"I hope you like dark, shadowed spaces then," Lea said.

Gong!

Margot struggled visibly with her decision.

Gong!

The fog rose to our knees, swirling faster and faster with every inch it rose.

Gong!

We were out of time!

"Margot, you have about three seconds."

Gong!

She glanced at me, her gaze murderous. "I won't be a bug forever, sorceress. And when I figure out a way to break out of this spell, I'm going to enjoy tearing you into tiny little pieces while you scream for mercy."

Gong!

The magic tugged at us, squeezing ethereal fingers of moist fog around our limbs.

Gong!

Lea and I shared a look and she nodded, letting

go of my shoulder. She started to spin, rotating so quickly I could no longer make out her individual features, and then was suddenly sucked down into the rising mist and disappeared.

Gong!

I looked at Margot, letting pity fill my gaze. "Your life's going to really suck. Hopefully, that parrot's gone when we get back. He looked pretty hungry."

Gong!

The magic wrung me out, yanked me around and burned against my skin until I hit the ground at Mythic Tea. I hit the tiled floor hard, lurching to stay on my feet.

Lea was in place, waiting with a special jar as Margot fell from the sky. She neatly captured the dropping cockroach and quickly screwed the top back on the jar. "Got her."

"You poked holes in the lid?" I asked my friend.

Lea got a confused look on her face. "Oops! Oh well..."

I laughed, shaking my head.

The front door flew open and Queen Sindra, surrounded by her soldiers and hundreds of Fairies, Elves and Sprites, flew through the door. I recognized the young woman with the ponytail who'd screamed "cockroach" in a crowded tea shop flying at her side in the signature garb of Sindra's guards.

"Where is she?" Sindra asked.

"Underneath the building where you found the kittens."

The queen inclined her head. "May nature bless and nourish you, Keeper Naida."

I inclined my head, feeling a weight leaving my chest as the queen went to release my friend. But even as I had the thought, my stomach twisted with despair. I still didn't have the artifact.

And the sun was very low on the horizon.

Rustin was almost out of time.

We walked into Croakies and I looked at Lea. "I can't believe I failed."

She must have seen the despair in my expression because she gave me a hug. "You didn't fail. You saved Sebille."

"And left Rustin to live a short life eating bug souffle as Mr. Slimy."

She patted my back and pulled away. "Rustin's fate was decided long before he showed up on your doorstep. Sometimes we just need to recognize when there are events beyond our control and make peace with it."

I nodded, only because she was looking at me like I was about to do a swan dive into a gallon of French vanilla, fudge ice cream.

Come to think of it, that sounded like an excellent idea.

"I'm heading home," she told me, handing me back the Book of Pages. Yeah, I'd shortened it because Book of Blank Pages was just too long to keep saying.

Efficiency, thy name is Naida. Naid? Na? N?

I locked the door behind Lea and trudged wearily across the floor. As I headed up the stairs to my apartment, I cast a look into the artifact library, frowning. First thing in the morning, I was going to find that hidden room the book had taken us to. I didn't like not knowing everything about the space I was living in.

Which is just hilarious, because I really knew very little about it. I just liked to tell myself I was the expert on the artifacts under my control.

A bright fluff of feathers sprang to life on top of the nearest shelves. "Shiver me timbers! It's the bawdy lass herself."

I instantly regretted having returned home long enough before dealing with Margot to put Wicked in my apartment and the sword with its mouthy counterpart back on the shelf. It had been a really long, day? Week? And I was too tired for SB's antics.

Opening the door to my apartment, I jolted to a stop as an unfamiliar scent, and an awareness of an unknown presence sounded alarm bells in my head.

I stilled, wishing I had Blackbeard's sword in my hand.

What a good idea!

I jerked my hand backward and the sword rose off the shelves with a clatter, smacking neatly into my palm a moment later.

I felt strangely pleased by my accomplishment until something else smacked into my back amid a spray of brightly hued feathers.

The parrot, who smelled like rum and pineapples, rose into the air in a clatter of feathers and landed crookedly on my shoulder.

I looked at him. "Have you been drinking?"

His beady eyes rolled unnaturally. "It's a tankard o' grog for every stout lad, but the lassies must sup tea...*hiccup*."

I rolled my eyes.

"It's about time you got here."

I jumped straight up in the air, the parrot's antics having distracted me from my invaded space. SB squawked with surprise, smacking me in the face with a wing as he rose into the air and fell back onto my shoulder, cackling drunkenly.

I lowered the sword with a shaky hand. It was LA. And standing behind her was her very attractive witch. "Hi, LA," I said with as much enthusiasm as I could muster. "Deg."

Despite my less-than-warm greeting, Deg smiled. "Hello, Keeper."

LA lifted an eyebrow at my inebriated shoulder bling. "I didn't know you had a parrot."

"Watch your *bleep*, lass. The ship is overrun with randy youth and *bleepin'* blackguards."

LA's other brow lifted.

"This is Sewer Beak," I told her. "I'm afraid he and the sword are an inseparable pair." I tugged a bright blue feather from my ear. "Much to my chagrin."

"We're running out of time," Deg said, striding closer. "If you want to save your friend."

My pulse spiked. "You found something?"

LA nodded. "It's the kittens."

I frowned. "What's the kittens?"

"They're the artifact," Deg said, his tone gentle.

Maybe it was my own personal form of resistance, or maybe I was too tired to think straight, but whichever it was, I felt the need to clarify. "The kittens? How is that possible?"

Deg reached into his pocket and pulled out the assortment of collars they'd taken off the rescued cats. "We've been focusing on these, thinking they were somehow tied to the artifact or the process of creating the artifact. But they're not. At least, not directly, they're simply..." He seemed to be struggling to express what he was thinking.

"Symbols," LA offered. "Reminders."

I shook my head, more confused than ever.

"That video you sent us," Deg said. "Did you

notice the glowing symbols on the air in front of each cat?"

"The sigils on their collars?" I asked.

"Not on the collars," Deg said. "None of the cats were wearing the collars at the time. It's almost as if the witches put the collars on the cats so they could remember which symbol was which."

"What are you saying?" I asked, rubbing my weary face. "If they weren't wearing the collars with the sigils..."

"The sigils are internal to each cat," LA told me. "They were glowing from inside the kittens' bodies."

My knees felt weak. I looked at Deg and he nodded affirmation.

I struggled for calm, my mind trying to figure out exactly what that meant. Finally, I asked, "Where does knowing that get us?"

Deg's face showed his excitement. He stepped forward, his hands coming up as he talked. "When they're together, the cats form an illuminory. A magic spell borne of light. That illuminory is your artifact."

I dropped my butt onto the arm of the nearest chair, suddenly too weary to stand. "You mean we've had the artifact all along?"

LA made a face. "Technically, we've had it since the kittens were rescued. But not really. Because, you see, that ritual you saw on the video, it wasn't the ritual to remove an essence. It was an attempt to replace a key element that makes the artifact work."

My head was starting to hurt. "I'm so confused."

LA and Deg shared a glance. Finally, LA sat down in a chair opposite me so we'd be at eye level. She reached out and clasped my hands. "Naida, the missing piece is Wicked."

21

NOT THEE

I just stared at them, so shocked I couldn't speak. It wasn't the idea that Wicked could be part of the artifact so much as the sheer impossibility that, if he was so very important, the Quillerans weren't trying harder to get him back.

"I've had him almost a year," I said to my friend.

LA nodded. "I know."

"Why haven't they ripped through here like cyclones to drag him back?"

LA looked to Deg for a response.

Deg shrugged. "I'm guessing whoever gave him to you warded him to ensure that he'd have to be given over willingly or something would happen that would negate his usefulness to them. When you refused to give him back to them willingly, they apparently tried to find a solution to the problem."

"By creating a symbol like the one he carries?" I guessed.

"Exactly."

The star! I thought back to the silver star emerging from the rubble of the ritual fire on the video. "I wonder if it worked."

"I'd say not," LA responded. "Since they're still trying to get you to give him to them of your own free will."

I shook my head, realizing that young Maude was much more formidable than I'd given her credit for. In one magical swoop, she'd ensured Wicked's safety and all but guaranteed that others wouldn't share Rustin's fate, while also creating an almost full-proof protection for herself.

If the Quillerans killed her, they'd never get their artifact back.

"How did you figure this out?" I asked my friends.

They shared a look and then nodded toward the stairs. "It's easier to show you," Deg said.

Nodding, LA added, "We want to try to save your friend."

M r. Wicked met us at the bottom of the stairs. He meowed a friendly greeting to LA and Deg, and encircled my ankles as I tried to move into the artifact library. "Hello, sweet boy," I cooed to him, scooping him up and nuzzling his soft fur. Whatever her motives, I couldn't help thinking how glad I was that Maude Quilleran decided to go against her family and bring him to me.

I turned to LA. "What did you want to show me?"

A chorus of meows filtered through the room, and one by one, the four other kittens from Wicked's litter emerged from underneath, behind, and inside the artifacts they'd been apparently exploring.

Wicked wriggled in my arms and I lowered him to the floor, where he immediately trotted off to scamper with his brothers and sisters. I turned a surprised look toward LA. "I thought you sent them away."

"We spread them far and wide. And then, the next morning they were back," Deg said.

LA nodded. "Turned up in my sanctuary, happy as you please."

I felt my eyes go wide. "How?"

"We have no idea. The people we entrusted them to said they were there one minute and gone the next."

We watched the kittens run around and wrestle

for a moment. Something warm blossomed inside my chest, and I wondered if the babies would ever find their furever homes. "What if the Quillerans spelled them to always return to them? What kind of life will they have?"

"But they didn't return to the witches," Deg said. "They showed back up at the sanctuary." He shook his head. "This is something else. I've seen it one other time. When an important ritual needed to be completed. The witches who were needed for the sacrament couldn't leave until it was complete. The magic protects itself."

"These kittens need to complete a ritual?" I asked the witch.

Deg frowned. "I believe that's what's going on here."

"But which ritual?" I asked.

"Hopefully the one we're about to perform," LA said with a bright smile. "I'd really like to get these babies homes where they'll be loved and appreciated."

I nodded. "Let's get to it then. Because, unless my lunar senses are completely off, the waning moon will rise within the hour."

The circle was set, drawn with salt and anchored by a ring of thick, white candles that flickered in the soft breeze from the overhead fans. As soon as Deg began to create his circle, the kittens stopped playing and wandered over to sprawl inside the ring of salt.

It was as if they knew exactly why they were there.

I eyed Mr. Wicked, my stomach churning with dread. What if joining the ritual changed him? What if it turned him away from me? I wasn't a witch. I was a special kind of sorceress, with limited powers that were focused almost entirely on managing artifacts.

He'd been meant to be a witch's familiar. If I'd doubted that before, I no longer did. Deg lit all the candles and Wicked positioned himself in the center of the circle, his litter mates taking their places around him like the spokes of a wheel.

The front door of my shop slammed closed, and I grabbed Blackbeard's sword, heading toward the front. I barely noticed when SB fluttered down to take his spot on my shoulder.

I didn't make it very far. Coming through the dividing door, I ran smack into a frantic, red-haired Sprite carrying a donut box.

Sebille was lucky I didn't skewer her.

"Oh, thank the goddess!" I pulled her into a hug

and, just for a beat, she allowed me to show her that small amount of affection.

Then she pulled away with a scowl. "We don't have time for that." She shoved the box into my hands. "He was locked up with me in the dungeon."

Mr. Slimy blinked up at me, his throat expanding and retracting as he gave a typically froggy glare.

"You don't have much time. Mother's army dispatched most of the Quillerans, but Jacob escaped."

I felt the blood leave my face. I'd relaxed knowing the enforcer was literally a bug in a jar, but I'd forgotten about the *other* most powerful Quilleran. I gave Sebille a look. "We'll talk later about what exactly you mean by, *dispatched*."

I had a moment to worry about Maude. The young witch had nothing to do with her family's schemes and had, in fact, done everything in her power to stop them. I hoped she hadn't gotten caught up in the Sprite Queen's retributive justice.

I hurried over and put the frog in the center of the circle. Slimy hopped around, croaking softly, but he never breached the energy buzzing at the boundaries of the sphere.

I looked at Sebille. "The moon?"

"On the cusp. You have maybe ten minutes."

I nodded. "Let's do it."

Deg glanced at Sebille. "Lights?"

Nodding, Sebille looked at me. "Will you be

okay? I promised mother I'd come to their new home. There's a..." She grimaced. "...meeting."

I smiled, knowing we'd have a lot to talk about later. "We've got this. Thanks for bringing Rustin back."

Sebille nodded and strode quickly to the wall beside the door, flipping the switch and plunging the artifact library into darkness lit only by flickering candlelight. I listened for the front door to close before turning back to the ritual preparations.

Deg stood just outside the circle, arms outstretched and eyes closed as he began to chant. Inside the salt barrier, the kittens went very still, their eyes becoming unfocused and their sleek gray fur darkening to black. At the center of each tiny chest, a shape emerged, glowing silver in the overwhelming darkness of the room.

The shapes of the various sigils glowed at the center of each kitten's chest. Deg and LA had been right. They were the symbols that had been represented on each kitten's collar.

Wicked stood in the exact center of the space, his body stiff and his gaze reflecting the flickering candlelight surrounding them.

I watched in awe as the fifth sigil appeared in the center of his furry chest. I immediately recognized it as a soul star sigil.

The silvery shape was a star in the center of a circle that was smaller in diameter than the points of the star. Silver flames leaped and danced from the circle, sizzling against the darkness surrounding the kittens.

As I watched in amazement, Wicked's sigil grew, rose from his chest, and lifted into the air, turning on its side to map the circumference of the circle Deg had drawn. The sigils on the other kittens rose from their chests too, lifting to attach themselves at the points of the star.

Deg's chanting grew louder, his words coming faster as the soul star began to spin. Each rotation revolved faster than the one that preceded it, until the soul star was spinning so quickly all I could see were the individual sigils, hanging like silvery gifts in midair.

LA gasped, drawing my gaze away from the spinning sigil.

A shape was rising from Mr. Slimy. Hunched and kneeling, Rustin slowly straightened until he stood in the very center of the whirling sigil.

I blinked, looking for Wicked, and found him lying on the floor beside me, sleeping soundly. One by one, the other four kittens left the circle and lay down next to him, falling into a deep sleep.

The kittens were okay. And the spell appeared to be working!

Deg's voice rose until it boomed through the artifact library, thundering off the walls and pinging over the gathered artifacts.

His hands moved quickly on the air and tiny, gold filaments grew in patterns from his rapidly dancing fingers. The filaments moved toward Rustin, who'd become more substantial, losing some of the ethereal quality I'd grown to recognize.

The witch's magic found Rustin's outstretched arms, folded around them like supple gold fabric, and spread over his torso. It rose to snug around his head and dropped to wrap around his feet and legs.

The filaments began to draw him from the circle, moving him inexorably toward the salt barrier.

He turned to me, a delighted smile finally curving his lips.

I smiled in return.

He was almost free!

A foul wind crashed through the space, blowing out several of the candles and ripping the delicate fabric of Deg's magic.

Rustin flinched, horror filling his eyes, and his gaze locked onto a spot behind Deg that was darker than night.

As I watched, the edges of the impossible blackness ripped away, burned by the orange, blue and gold flames of magic.

The foul, sulfurous stench spun in whirlwinds around us, blowing the salt to break the circle and extinguishing the rest of the ritual candles.

The magical light of the artifacts filtered through the room, the magic deciding it was time to return.

A man stepped from the circle of fire he'd created on the air.

Jacob Quilleran.

"Deg, behind you!" LA screamed.

Deg's hands lifted as he spun, and a wrist-thick stream of magic burst from them, spearing directly toward Jacob Quilleran.

He threw up his hands and spread a cloak of blue energy between him and Deg's power, holding it off as LA sent her own burst of energy into the mix.

Jacob stumbled back a few steps, but his magic held. After a moment, he managed to push Deg and LA back, regaining the space he'd lost and then some.

He eyed the kittens, a lust for power filling his cold, handsome face.

I clutched the sword, "Don't even think about it, Quilleran!" I yelled, my voice booming around the room as the power of the sword filled my veins.

His response was to smile at me, the sight turning my blood to ice. "You've interfered with my family one too many times Keeper. I'm here to put an end to your interference and retrieve what's mine."

Moving in front of the pile of kittens, I lifted the sword, holding it out in front of me in both hands. "You're not getting these kittens."

Roiling blue energy filled both his outstretched

palms. "Oh, but I am. And when I'm done with you, I'm going to release my enforcer from the little four-dimensional glamour you put on her and all of your friends will die."

Yikes! He knew about that?

A screech sounded behind me, followed by the sound of something rolling through the dark.

Jacob wasn't distracted by the sound. He drew his hand back and threw the energy at me.

Acting strictly on instinct, I lifted the sword and met the bolt with the blade, shattering it into pieces and sending SB into the air in a flurry of feathers and squawking.

The force of the strike ricocheted through me, making my teeth and knees clack together.

Blackbeard's sword appeared unharmed.

LA flew at Jacob with a long blade, energy pulsing along its glinting edge. She threw herself into the air and did a somersault, landing behind him and slicing upward with the deadly blade.

He jerked sideways and the blade slipped between his arm and his body, then he slammed her in the face with an energy-powered backhand, sending her flying to crash against something that clattered loudly to the concrete floor.

Finding the mirror at my back, I slapped my palm against the glass and yelled, "Sebille!" I prayed she'd hear me and come in time.

Deg had been chanting since Jacob discombobulated his ritual, his fingers dancing rapidly on the air. He'd created an impressive golden web. With a final magical word, he threw it at the other witch before Jacob could react.

The web hit Quilleran and wrapped quickly around him, yanking his arms to his sides and encompassing him in a seemingly unbreakable embrace.

Jacob staggered sideways, his energy flaring out from his hands and burning along the web with what I at first thought was little effect.

But a heartbeat later, the webbing fell away from him, disappearing into the air as it sifted downward.

"Sebille!" I tried again, my desperate gaze falling to the kittens near my feet.

Deg lifted his hands again but didn't get a chance to try another spell. Jacob's voice boomed around the room as a power word burst from his lungs, sending the other witch flying away from him to join LA on the artifact-littered floor.

Then Jacob turned to me.

My pulse pounded so hard that I was afraid I might pass out. But I faced him calmly, the sword still gripped in my hand. It burned my palm, the energy building there impatient to be spent.

SB flapped his wings, dancing from side to side on my shoulder. "Aye, ye blackguard grab yer sword. Or blood will be spent ye can ill afford."

I felt my lips curve upward as a calm came over

me. I swung the blade in a testing motion, slashing it through the magic-drenched air and stepping toward Jacob.

He shoved his hands into his pockets and waited, a smug look on his evil, handsome face.

"Ye might think ye'll know, ye might think ye'll see, but Blackbeard's blade is on to thee."

I flashed forward, my feet moving so fast I didn't even have time to think about moving, and swung the blade.

Jacob's smug expression fell away, and a look of surprise replaced it. He looked down at the ribbon of blood seeping through his shirt.

With a roar, he grabbed for some energy.

"Ye scurvy blackguard think ye see. But none can track the speed. Not thee."

The blade slashed from stem to stern, opening up a long, shallow cut that spilled more blood the length of Jacob's torso.

"Not thee."

It flashed again. And again. And again.

As Jacob dropped to his knees, I lowered the sword to my side, suddenly exhausted beyond belief.

"Not thee," I murmured, staggering backward and dropping the blade.

Sebille stepped out of the darkness, her fiery red hair like a beacon. "Is this what you were looking for?"

I took the book, panting with exhaustion. "The kittens?" I asked my friend.

"Safe."

I nodded, holding the book perched on my open palm as the pages started to flicker. They sped and sped until they found the exact page I'd been looking for. Then they stopped and I looked down at the familiar image of the clock tower.

I glanced toward Jacob. "You'll hate it here, which makes me smile. It's not exactly Hell, but it's pretty darn close." I reached down and grabbed one of his bloody hands, lifting it and pressing it against the image.

I watched the magic grab him, yank him off the ground, and tug him into the book, his bloody palm print seeping into the page along with him.

Then I reached out and ripped the page from the book, tearing it into a hundred tiny pieces and setting it to flame with my piddly magic before I let my knees buckle and carry me to the ground.

Sebille took the book from me and helped me to my feet. "Come on Keeper. I'm going to make you a cup of tea."

My head pounded and my vision swam. "My friends..."

"They're fine. I called Lea. She'll make sure they get any care they need."

I nodded, licking my dry lips. "Sebille?"

"What?" she asked as she supported me up the steps.

"You're not being nice to me, are you?"

She stiffened against me. "If you tell anybody I'll deny it."

I grinned. "Your secret's safe with me."

She helped me through the door and over to my bed. I saw with a smile that Wicked's pillow was dented by his soft little body.

There was also a kitten on *my* pillow. And the rest of the bed was covered with the other three. I sighed. "Couch it is then."

Sebille shook her head but didn't try to talk me out of it. She got me settled on the couch. Even covered me with a blanket, and then went to make me some tea that would hopefully pull the ache from my head.

Then I had a sudden, horrible thought. I jerked upright, forgetting about the headache in my panic and grasping my head with a groan. "Frog's cankles!"

"Lie still," Sebille barked at me.

I lay back down, my hand covering my eyes as they tried to spin out of my head. "What happened to Rustin? Is he out of the frog?"

Sebille handed me my cup. Her funny-looking freckled face scrunched with unhappiness. "I'm afraid not. Quilleran's interference stopped the ritual before he made it out."

Tears burned my eyes. "Poor Rustin."

Sebille stepped away. "We'll find another way. Your friends were talking downstairs. They're already working on it."

I nodded, sniffling as I raised the cup to my lips. I held tight to her reassurance, which was a rare gem because she so infrequently bothered with such things. I made myself a promise that I would find a way to release Rustin.

He deserved a chance at the life his family stole from him. In the meantime, I guessed I could keep a frog and a cat. Lots of people dealt with far more animal sidekicks than that.

The rim of the teacup touched my lips, and I stilled. Looking up at Sebille, I narrowed my gaze. "You didn't use an infuser on this, did you?"

Her laughter was singularly annoying. Especially since it went on for several minutes. And in the end, seeing a particular glint in her eye, I was afraid to drink my tea.

22

ALL WRAPPED UP

I stood under the bleachers and looked around, seeing the torn grass and scorched metal from our battle with Margot. The memory sat heavy on my chest. Not because of Margot, but because of what the incident had set into motion for Maude Quilleran.

No one had spoken to her since the night Queen Sindra's army liberated Sebille and Mr. Slimy from captivity, capturing Felicity, Candace, and several Quilleran cousins before Jacob Quilleran managed to escape their net.

The Quillerans, including the cockroach in a magic jar, were currently cooling their heels, or the cockroach equivalent, in a special prison run by The Société of Dire Magic. Miracle of miracles, I'd learned that the Société had offices somewhere in the States, although nobody could tell me where they were.

I was thinking Area 51 maybe. I mean, why not?

And Jacob. The page in the book was still torn out. It hadn't reappeared. Using my knowledge of how magic works, and some careful investigation by Lea, I was going with, he was still wandering around in the fog under that dang clock, which never quite reached the bewitching hour of Midnight anymore.

Good.

He could stay there for eternity as far as I was concerned.

As for Rustin. Well. I'd had another dream about him the night before. He'd seemed resigned to his fate, only asking that I watch out for his cousin Maude. He'd assured me she was one of the few good Quilleran witches.

I didn't doubt that at all.

Which was why I was currently standing under the bleachers holding the teen's cell phone, hoping I could see her and maybe offer to help.

But I'd been there for over an hour, and with every passing moment, I realized it had been stupid to think I could run into her there.

She was probably hiding out somewhere, believing she was in the Société's crosshairs. I just hoped she was okay because I really wanted to fulfill that promise to Rustin. I hadn't been able to do much else to help him.

Sighing my resignation, I placed the phone on the concrete surrounding the central support leg of the bleachers, as Maude had asked me to do.

I'd probably never know the answers to the other questions in my mind. I'd have to learn to deal with that.

At least I'd fulfilled my task of finding and securing the artifact I'd been assigned. The kittens had given up their special sigils the night we'd tried to bring Rustin back. Though the ritual had been interrupted, dooming poor Rustin to spending the remainder of his life as a frog, the kittens had fulfilled their task, and whatever had impelled them to stay together was gone.

With the Quillerans spread far and wide, I thought they might finally be safe. Lea had declared it was time she took a true familiar and claimed the smallest kitten for her own, a sweet-faced little girl she'd named Hex.

LA had taken the remaining three kittens back with her, stating that Deg and her other witch friend, Mandy, might take two of them. She'd also been nursing a quiet confidence about the third. I hoped that meant she was thinking of keeping her. It would be fun if we could keep all the babies close enough to see each other on a regular basis.

I started off toward my car, which was parked in the exact same spot it had been the night we'd run from the enforcer. I know this because the perfect outline of my little VW bug was burned into the High School parking lot.

No doubt from powerful cloaking Fae magics.

It felt like I had a duty to park my car in that perfect outline. It would seem ungrateful not to.

"Naida?"

I jerked to a stop, spinning on my heel.

Young Maude stood in the grass several feet behind me, hugging herself and looking at me as if I might pull out Blackbeard's sword and smite her with it.

First of all, that wasn't even a possibility. Not only was I done smiting people for a long, long time, but after too many hours spent carting SB around on my shoulder, I was still pulling parrot feathers out of my hair and clothes. I had no desire to revisit that roller-coaster fun ride any time soon.

"Maude. You're okay?"

She nodded, rubbing her arms as if she were cold. "I'm with...family."

I understood she didn't want to tell me more than that. She probably didn't fully trust that I wouldn't turn her in to The Société of Dire Magic. "Good. I'm glad you're safe. The kittens are safe too. And Wicked would love to see you if you ever want to come for a visit."

She nodded, the ghost of a smile finally finding her pretty face. "I'd love that."

We stood in silence for a few beats and then I pointed toward the bleachers. "I put your phone where you told me. Thanks, by the way, for your help. I'm only sorry we couldn't save Rustin."

Maude frowned. "Don't worry about that. I actually have somebody working on it. We have his body and the original artifact, and we hope to extract him soon."

I felt my brows climbing up my forehead. "You do? But where...how?"

She shook her head. "I can't say. I'm sorry. You understand?"

I hesitated only briefly before nodding. "Of course. I'm just happy to hear you might be able to help him." I had a flash of understanding and suddenly knew who had the artifact and how they planned to help Rustin. I also realized why the Quillerans had been trying to create a substitute for the original artifact with the kittens. They'd probably never actually had Balthire's creation in their hands.

If I wasn't mistaken, Eglund Balthire's mystery woman, the inspiration for the original well-meaning artifact, was alive and well and likely had his ritual notes to work with.

That was really good news for Rustin and answered a lot of my questions too, which was a bonus. And, since the artifact was, arguably, with its original owner, I could leave it right where it was. No need to rescue it and ensconce it in the artifact library.

Maude nodded, looking relieved. "Well, I should get going. I just wanted to tell you I was all right. And to thank you for trying to help Rustin. That means a lot to...us."

I shook my head. "I failed. I can't accept your thanks."

"Only because Pops stopped you. It's not your fault."

I shrugged, praying Maude didn't ask what happened to her father.

She didn't. "Goodbye, Naida."

"Goodbye, Maude." I watched her turn and walk a few feet away before calling out to her again. "Maude?"

She half-turned. "Yes?"

"Tell Madeline I said hey."

Shock filled her Quilleran yellow gaze, and I realized she'd come into her true magic, losing the blue eyes of her birth to the color of the family magic. Which meant, when she'd spelled Wicked to protect him from her family, she'd only been a novice witch. The thought was daunting. She and her Aunt Madeline were more alike than I'd ever suspected.

Both scary powerful.

Then she gave me a crooked smile. "I'll do that, Keeper. If I happen to run into her."

I turned away, grinning, and headed back toward Croakies with a much lighter heart.

The End

READ MORE ENCHANTING INQUIRIES

Did you enjoy **Tea & Croakies**? If so, you might want to check out Book 2 of Enchanting Inquiries, Fortune Croakies.

Please enjoy Chapter One of **Fortune Croakies**, my gift to you!

I wish my job as a magical librarian was just about shuffling books and shushing people from behind a desk. Alas, the magic I wrangle requires a bit more than shuffling and shushing. And to make things worse, I have a frog and a cat, and I have no idea how to use them!

Sure, I understand, we all have bills to pay. Personally, I could use a bit of extra cash too. But I'm pretty sure I wouldn't kill for it. At least...not without dark magic influence. And that's exactly the problem.

Dark. Magic. Influence.

My first challenge for the day is finding that artifact and putting it under lock and key before it kills anybody else.

My second challenge is figuring out how to deal with a bossy frog and a pushy cat.

Which of the two do you suppose will give me the bigger headache?

Yeah. That's what I think too. The frog and cat are going to be the death of my sanity.

Maybe I should put them under lock and key too.

FORTUNE CROAKIES

It isn't every day that you find yourself staring at a frog's fat butt bulging out of a sink drain. I would have felt better if I believed it would never happen again, but given the facts of my very strange life, I figured it definitely would.

Sighing, I have the squishy bulk a tentative poke with my finger, earning a forlorn, "Ribbit!" for my efforts. Something trickled downward, hitting my cheek and dripping down to the paper towel I had draped under my head to keep "under the sink" cooties off my hair.

I realized, too late, what had just dripped on me.

"Argh!" I shoved out from under the sink and bent over while grabbing frantically for more paper towel to wipe frog pee off my cheek. "I can't believe it!"

The figure lounging against my refrigerator grinned. "You shouldn't poke a stressed frog, Naida."

I glared at the source of almost all my problems.

Okay, I know I previously said that about Mr. Wicked, my adorable kitten who was probably better at being an artifact keeper than I was. But I'd reassessed the players and decided Rustin Quilleran, former witch and current frog squatter, was definitely more trouble than my sweet little kitten.

I mean, Wicked was curled up on his pillow, purring happily.

Rustin was driving a fat frog bus that got itself jammed in my drain and peed on my face.

I'll let you do the math.

"Not funny. You need to keep a better lock on the contents of your bladder."

His grin widened. "I think you have a mistaken view of my ability to control your wedged friend," he told me. "I'm just a passenger on that particular bus."

Which, normally I'd be happy about. I mean, when Rustin had gotten stuck in the frog because of a spell his terrible family had performed, I'd felt terrible. We'd tried everything to get him out of there. But, in the end, the evil Jacob Quilleran had interfered, making certain poor Rustin didn't escape the fate Jacob had locked him into.

I still hadn't found out why Rustin's Uncle Jacob had felt the need to lock him in a frog.

Rustin wasn't being very forthcoming with the information.

I hurried past him, into my bathroom, where I put soap onto the wet paper towel and scrubbed my cheek until I was in danger of removing a layer of skin cells along with the frog pee.

"What are you doing here, then? Standing there laughing isn't helping at all."

Rustin shrugged. "I was bored. Your life is generally good for a few laughs. I'm happy to report that this morning has been no exception."

I barely resisted zapping him with my almost worthless keeper magics. I pretty much had only enough umph in my zapper to curl someone's hair or make them pee themselves.

Trust me when I tell you I'd had enough of making stuff pee for the day.

Flinging the soiled paper towel into the trash, I glared at him. "I'm so glad I could entertain."

"Me too." His grin never wavered.

A part of me was happy to see it. I'd been so worried that Rustin would lose his humanity because of his enforced incarceration in the frog. But his cousin Maude and his very powerful Aunt Madeline had been working on reversing the spell. They hadn't managed yet to free him. But they'd created a metaphysical barrier between Mr. Slimy's — a.k.a. the frog's — consciousness and Rustin's so he could maintain his power, brain capacity, and humanity... basically his soul.

That was as good a result as we could have hoped for under the circumstances.

Even though that meant, as Mr. Slimy's unhappy owner, I was also the temporary owner of an ethereally handsome and snarky witch who was stuck inside a frog.

And you thought I was kidding about the challenges of my life.

The bell jangled downstairs in my book store and I glanced at my stuck amphibian.

"Ribbit." His sticky tongue snapped out and snagged a massive fly that had tried to make a break for the window above the sink.

Sucker!

I looked at Rustin. "Keep an eye on the fat, green bus. I have to go see who's downstairs."

He nodded, casting what appeared to be a fond glance toward Mr. Slimy.

I shook my head. How anybody could be fond of a frog was beyond me.

Although, I realized as I bounced down the steps to the first floor, that I'd formed some sort of attachment that went beyond disgust. I almost dreaded the day Madeline managed to find a way to extract her nephew. I was going to miss him.

Unlocking the door that separated the book store

from the artifact library behind me, I blinked in surprise.

Had I just had a Freudian moment? Was I going to miss the witch? Or the frog?

I shrugged, shoving the question aside for another time. I figured it would be an easy choice.

I mean, one of them just peed on me.

My friend Lea was standing in front of the door with something large and red balanced on her hands. She was holding it out in front of her like an offering, a wide smile on her pretty round face. "We have apples!"

My mouth fell open. "That's an apple? I thought it was a giant ball or something."

I wandered toward her, my gaze locked on the enormous, shiny fruit.

She was just about dancing with excitement. "Fairies!" she squealed happily.

Lea ran an herbalist shop next door and she had a giant greenhouse out behind her shop. The greenhouse had recently had a large influx of Fae when the Quilleran clan had burned their homes in the Enchanted Forest...long story...to the ground.

Everyone knows that one of the side benefits of having Fairies was that, if you're on good terms with them, they blessed your garden.

What I'm not sure many people knew, including me, was exactly *how* blessed it became.

I lifted an awed look to Lea's overjoyed face. "I didn't even know you had apple trees."

"I didn't," she exclaimed happily. "Until a couple of weeks ago. They're already five feet tall." She gave in and did the little happy dance she'd been trying not to do. "I can't believe these apples. And you should taste them. Sweet, crisp and perfect." She rolled the apple around on top of her hand so I could see its perfect skin.

"That's amazing!" I agreed, laughing. "And I'm more than a little jealous right now."

Her expression softened. "This is for you. Queen Sindra insisted. I'm to provide as many of these and the peaches she's currently nurturing as you'd like. To thank you for saving her daughter."

I took the apple she handed me and barely kept from doing a little happy dance of my own. "Sweet Caroline," I said, licking my lips.

The front door opened again and a strange-looking creature with fire-red hair, a pale face covered in freckles, and large pointed ears stepped into my shop.

I would have expelled her immediately if I could have. Not because she was dangerous. But because she looked even crankier than usual and I was on an apple high. I didn't want her to bring me down.

Lea turned to my city Sprite and gave her an impulsive hug. "Good morning, Sebille."

Sebille narrowed her iridescent green gaze suspiciously. "Have you been licking your frog again?"

Lea giggled. "Wally doesn't have any psychedelic grease. He's a bullfrog."

Sebille rolled her eyes, a fairly regular habit with her. "Stop smiling you two, it's annoying." She shuffled over to the counter to plunk her enormous, ugly bag on the shelf beneath.

Lea and I scanned her strange garb, which currently included black, red and white striped knee socks that ended in shiny red "wicked witch of the west" shoes, and a dark green dress with tight sleeves that hooked over each of her thumbs and skimmed the tops of her strange socks.

She'd plaited her long hair into two braids that separated around her oversized ears.

I decided to take the bull by the...erm...braids. What can I tell you? Once you've been peed on by a frog, you really have nothing left to lose. "What's got your granny panties in a twist today?" I asked my assistant.

She glared through the bangs she'd been recently growing out. They hung into her eyes more often than not and gave her a bad-tempered imp look. "I'm being evicted."

Lea and I shared a horrified look, probably both thinking the same thing.

What if she wants to move in with one of us?

Lea poked my arm and I shook my head. "Nope,

not happening. I'm already babysitting a smart-mouthed witch ghost and a frog that jams himself into the sink drain and then pees on my face."

Lea frowned, seemingly trying to untangle the imagery I'd just spewed in her direction, then shook her head. "I've got you beat. I have five...maybe seven..." She cocked her head. "I keep losing count. I have hundreds of Fae in my garden. I'm Fae'd out."

A forceful sigh yanked our attention back toward Evicta the Homeless Sprite. "You're both heartless shrews."

Lea shrugged and I nodded. If keeping my space grouchy Sprite free made me a shrew, then I'd happily wear the badge.

"Why'd you get evicted?" I asked Sebille, walking over to place my head-sized apple on the counter. I needed to take it upstairs where I could happily hoard it until it was totally consumed. But I needed to make sure Sebille's search for a new home took her in the right direction.

Namely, any direction but mine.

She gave the apple a cursory look, no doubt used to giant apples since she was a Sprite. "I might have over-vaped and turned one of Devard's best customers...temporarily...into a slug."

Devard was the owner of the vapery across the street.

When Sebille saw the horror on our faces, she held up her hands. "Just for a blip. The guy hardly even had time to slime a path to the door before he was back again. Besides, he didn't even know he was a slug until that stupid woman with the frizzy hair started screaming like a Banshee."

I frowned. "You mean the Banshee who lives across the street?"

"Yeah," Sebille agreed, warming to her complaints. "What's with all that screaming anyway? Don't those weirdos have anything better to do?"

Lea and I shared a look.

Sebille had taken an apartment over the vapery and she spent most of her free time creating and then sucking special vapes made with...unique... herbs. She was known, on occasion, to share her special concoctions with others. Those occasions were generally problematic.

I'm pretty sure I'd climbed the fire escape on the side of the building the one time I'd tried Sebille's special vape. There are rumors that I'd tried to ride a large crow, insisting it was my own personal dragon.

Shredded crow-psyche aside, I'd almost died that night.

Yeah. You heard that right. I just made it about me.

That crow should have known better than to stick around when I hit the roof. He should have seen the madness in my eyes and disembarked toot suite! The fact that he hung around, cawing at me as if he were laughing at my attempts to saddle him, made him just as much to blame for what happened as I was.

And no, I didn't hurt the crow. Except for his pride.

I'm pretty sure those feathers on his head will grow back.

Lea suddenly decided she had to go. "Um...I'll see you ladies later."

The door was slamming shut behind her as my gaze found Sebille's. "It shouldn't be hard to find another place," I told my assistant.

She shrugged. "Not one I can afford. My place is really cheap." She gave me a slightly hostile look, as if the salary I was paying her was part of the conspiracy to see her homeless.

I bit back a defensive retort and patted her on the shoulder. "We'll find you a great place. But right now, I have something I need to do upstairs." I grabbed my apple and headed toward the stairs.

"Naida?"

I stopped in the doorway. "Yes?"

She fidgeted with the stapler and calculator, her gaze avoiding mine. "Do you think I could sleep here just until I find a place?"

My heart broke a little at the sight of her. She was so embarrassed to ask. And despite my cocky response to the news she'd been evicted, I knew I couldn't let her hit the streets.

I swallowed the enormous lump in my throat

and nodded. "Sure. But maybe it won't come to that. There have to be a ton of cute studio apartments in Enchanted."

She grimaced, nodding. "Thanks."

I spun on my heel and made my way back up the stairs, my step a lot heavier than it had been before. Lifting my chin, I squared my shoulders. I'd find Sebille a place to live if it was the last thing I did.

But, in the meantime, Sebille's snarky comment to Lea had inspired me.

And I had a frog to grease.

Check out the entire series here: https://samcheever. com/books/#enchanting

ALSO BY SAM CHEEVER

If you enjoyed **Tea & Croakies**, you might also enjoy these other fun mystery series by Sam. To find out more, visit the **BOOKS** page at www.samcheever.com:

Reluctant Familiar Paranormal Mysteries
Yesterday's Paranormal Mysteries
Gainfully Employed Mysteries
Silver Hills Cozy Mysteries
Country Cousin Mysteries

ABOUT THE AUTHOR

USA Today and WSJ Bestselling Author Sam Cheever writes contemporary and paranormal mystery and suspense, creating stories that draw you in and keep you eagerly turning pages. Known for writing great characters, snappy dialogue, and unique and exhilarating stories, Sam is the award-winning author of 80+ books.

To learn more about Sam and her work, visit her at one of her online hotspots:
www.samcheever.com
samcheever@samcheever.com